THE NANCY DREW FILES™ CASE · 34

VANISHING ACT

Carolyn Keene

AN ARCHWAY PAPERBACK
Published by SIMON & SCHUSTER
New York   London   Toronto   Sydney   Tokyo   Singapore

An Archway paperback
first published in Great Britain
by Simon & Schuster Ltd in 1992
A Paramount Communications Company

Simon & Schuster Ltd
West Garden Place
Kendal Street
London W2 2AQ

Simon & Schuster of Australia Pty Ltd
Sydney

A CIP catalogue record for this book is
available from the British Library

ISBN 0-671-71650-2

Printed and bound in Great Britain by
HarperCollins Manufacturing, Glasgow

VANISHING
ACT

Chapter
One

Nancy, get in here right away! The show's about to start!"

Nancy Drew glanced at her watch. "I'm ten minutes early, Bess," she called out through the open window of her car, smiling. Nancy slid out of her Mustang and started toward her friend. Bess Marvin was standing in the doorway to her house, almost dancing with impatience.

"Come *on*, come *on!*" she said as Nancy sauntered up the path. "George is already here. Do you want a soda or something? No, never mind. I'll get you one when there's a commercial. I don't want to miss even a *second* of this show."

"Well, you're certainly not going to," George Fayne commented dryly as Nancy followed Bess into the living room. George was Bess's first cousin, and she and Bess were Nancy's two best friends. "You have time to get fifty sodas if you want. I'm glad you're here, Nancy. It's too much for one person to deal with Bess when she's like this."

"I'm glad to be here, too," Nancy said. "I've been feeling lonely with Ned away."

Ned Nickerson, Nancy's boyfriend, had returned to Emerson College earlier that day after a long weekend at home. Nancy was delighted when Bess had asked her over. Now she wouldn't have to spend the whole evening missing Ned.

Bess wasn't listening to anything they were saying. "I just hope you programmed this thing right, George," she fretted, gesturing at the VCR. "This is one tape I *have* to have in my collection."

"Bess, no one can see if you keep standing in front of the TV," said George. "Just sit down and relax. It's all going to be fine. You'll have your permanent record of Jesse Slade to put in your hope chest. Not that it'll do you any good— unless he suddenly returns one day."

Bess sighed. "I still can't believe he's gone. My biggest idol—the greatest rock star in the world —gone. How could anyone have disappeared like that? Especially anyone so famous?"

"I wasn't as big a fan of his as you were, but I

do understand. It seems unreal to me, too," George said. "I can't believe three years have passed since he disappeared."

Three years. Nancy thought. It *did* seem impossible. Three years before, Jesse Slade had been on the way to becoming the biggest rock star in the country. He'd been only nineteen then, but he had already cut two albums—composing all the music, writing all the lyrics, singing and playing, and producing. The first had gone gold, and the second platinum.

Jesse Slade had also been the only rock musician in history to have six singles in a row reach number one on the charts. He'd won two Grammy Awards. And on top of that, he'd been gorgeous—with long dark brown hair, coal black eyes, and a sad, haunting smile that drove his fans wild.

"He was talented, Bess—I'll give you that," George was saying now.

"But I didn't like him because he was *talented!*" Bess protested. "And not because he was so cute, either. It was just— Well, there was something about him," she finished helplessly.

Nancy knew what Bess was trying to say. His talent and his looks weren't all that had made Jesse Slade so popular. He'd had a warm and intimate quality that made his songs seem as if they were a private conversation between each fan and himself. Jesse also made each fan feel as if he needed him or her.

3

Then, at the height of his popularity, Jesse Slade had vanished—without a trace.

No one knew *how* it had happened. Jesse and his band had been the main attraction at a huge outdoor concert on a beach in California. Jesse had been onstage for about forty minutes when he'd announced that he was going to take a short break.

He'd never been seen again.

The rest of the band was onstage when he'd disappeared. None of them had seen him vanish. Neither had anyone on the crew. And neither had any of the thousands of fans who'd been watching the concert. It seemed impossible—but he'd vanished and never come back.

But he'd never been forgotten—not by his millions of loyal fans, and not by the music industry. Both of his albums were still in the Top 100, and not a day went by that he wasn't mentioned in the music press. He might have disappeared, but the mystery of his disappearance had kept his career alive.

"It's even too much of a mystery for me," Nancy mused aloud. "I was just thinking about Jesse," she said in answer to George's quizzical look.

The show the girls were going to watch that night would kick off a week-long celebration of Jesse Slade on TV Rock, a cable music-video station whose nickname was TVR. "Who's hosting the segment tonight, Bess?" Nancy asked, her thoughts returning to the present.

"Dan Kennedy," answered her friend. "He's in charge of the whole week." Dan Kennedy was one of TVR's most popular veejays. "Tomorrow TVR's going to be interviewing the rest of the guys in Jesse's band, and the day after they'll go out to Jesse's hometown to talk to people who knew him when he was growing up. And they're going to play one of Jesse's songs every hour on the hour, and—"

"And they're going to have a seance to try to find Jesse, aren't they?" George put in.

"George!" Bess protested. "How can you joke like that?"

"Well, how can you make such a fuss about a guy you've never met and never will get the chance to meet?" George countered. "I mean, I know he was incredible, and I've heard of long-distance love, but don't you think this is a little *too* long-distance? Like so long-distance it's nonexistent?"

"Oh, you're just—Wait, it's starting!" Bess said excitedly. She plunked herself down in front of the TV. "George, hand me that brush. I have to look my best."

"Right, Bess," George grumbled, but she gave her the brush anyway.

The TVR logo flashed on the screen. "TV *Rock!*" an echoing voice boomed. "Where the party never stops-ops-ops-ops-ops—"

5

"Oh, come on, get going!" said Bess. "We *know* it's TV Rock!"

Then Dan Kennedy strolled in front of the camera and sat down. "Hi, teen angels," he said with a grin, pushing his curly blond hair out of his eyes. "Like the shirt? A crazed fan just handed it to me on my way in." He pointed down at his T-shirt, which said "Evil Picnickers Unlock Secrets of the Pyramids" in huge black letters dripping with red. "I don't know exactly what it means," Dan Kennedy went on. "Maybe you do. Send your suggestions to me, along with ten dollars. When I have enough money, I'll retire!" he finished brightly. "Then I can devote my time to figuring out what my clothes are trying to tell me.

"Anyway"—Dan Kennedy's face became serious—"tonight marks the beginning of Jesse Slade Week. As most of you know, Jesse took off, or was taken off, or something, three years ago tonight. We're going to be remembering him at TVR this week—not that anyone who ever had anything to do with Jesse could really forget him. Tonight we're bringing you a very special tape of Jesse's last concert. TVR just uncovered it. It was thought to have been lost in a fire but was found mostly intact. We hope you'll be as moved by it as we were."

There was a burst of guitar music, and onto the screen flashed a picture of Jesse Slade bent over his guitar. It cut to a shot of screaming fans leaping out of their seats at a concert, and then to another still of Jesse, vaulting through the air in one of the leaps that had been his onstage trademark.

"Jesse Slade—the man, the musician, and the mystery," came Dan Kennedy's voice-over. "Will we ever know what happened to him?"

"Nope," said George. Bess kicked her ankle.

"On this night three years ago, Jesse Slade played his last concert," Dan continued. "Tonight, we're bringing you that concert again."

The screen went to dark. At first Nancy wasn't sure what was happening. Then she realized that the screen was dark because the stage was dark. She could hear the occasional sounds of an expectant crowd—a catcall, throats clearing, a few bursts of applause. Then a tiny beam of light flashed onto the center of the stage.

A drum began beating—slowly at first, then fast. The beam of light grew larger—larger—larger. Now Nancy could see the huge outdoor stage that had been set up dramatically close to a cliff at the edge of the Pacific Ocean. Behind the stage, a fading sunset was a background for the black water.

Then Jesse Slade walked slowly to center stage —and the crowd went wild.

"Show the fans!" George said. "I love footage of fans."

As if in answer, the camera panned slowly over the crowd: a sweat-drenched boy waving a hand-painted sign that said "Jesse Forever"; a girl screaming hysterically and jumping up and down, tears of emotion streaming down her face; a forest of hands clapping rhythmically in the air as Jesse picked up a guitar and began the notes of his opening song.

For the next half hour the three girls watched the screen in total silence. Jesse stepped forward and held up his hand. Gradually the crowd grew quiet.

"I'm going to do one more," Jesse said, "and then I'm turning the stage over to my band for a while. They're pretty good, too, you know." There was a ripple of laughter from the crowd. "This one's from my first album," Jesse said, picking up his guitar. "I think most of you know it."

And he began to play the first bars of "Goodbye, Sweet Life."

Bess gasped, and a chill ran down Nancy's spine. "I'd forgotten that was the last song he played," Nancy said.

"Me, too," Bess answered. "It's creepy, isn't it?"

"Totally," said George. "It's almost as if he'd planned it or something. I wonder if . . ." Her voice trailed off, and the three girls fell silent again.

"Goodbye, sweet life," Jesse sang.

"You won't be missed . . .

"It's much too late to cry. . . ."

The crowd fell utterly silent for the next few minutes. Then, abruptly, the song ended. "See you in ten!" Jesse shouted jauntily as he strode off the stage to tumultuous applause.

"And that's *it?*" George said. "He doesn't come back?"

"No," Bess said sadly. "Well, I guess I'll get us a soda now. I don't care much about watching his band." Sighing, she pulled herself to her feet and went out to the kitchen.

Nancy picked up a magazine and began idly leafing through it as Jesse's backup band began to play. She wasn't really interested in them, either. She put down the magazine as Bess strolled back into the room carrying a six-pack of diet soda. On the television screen, Jesse's bass player was jamming with his guitarist. "How about switching channels for a little while, Bess?" she said. "This is getting kind of—"

Suddenly she broke off. What was that?

A strange flicker of movement in one corner of the screen had just caught her eye.

"What's the matter?" George asked.

"Something at the back of the stage," Nancy answered. "See, in that corner—there. Wait! What's going on?"

9

The back of the stage was dark and shadowy now. But Nancy was sure she wasn't imagining things.

She'd just seen what looked like it could have been a body. It was hurtling over the cliff beside the stage!

Chapter

Two

"Bess, stop the tape!" Nancy said excitedly. "Did you see that?"

"See what?" Bess asked. "What are you talking about?"

"I think I saw someone fall off the cliff! I have to check it again!"

"That's impossible! Why would something like that happen during a concert? Anyway, I didn't notice anything. Can't it wait?" Bess asked. "I want to watch the end. And I want the *whole* tape, not just part of it."

"Okay," Nancy agreed reluctantly. But she was so eager to check out what she'd seen that the rest of the show dragged for her. At last Dan Kennedy's face appeared on the screen again.

"We'll have more tomorrow night on Jesse," he said. "Same time, same place, same Dan. And now, take a look at the new video by the Same, ours exclusively on TVR—"

George leaned over and snapped off the TV. "Okay, Nan. What did you see?" she asked.

Quickly Nancy rewound the tape to the point where she thought she'd seen the body fall. At first she couldn't find the exact footage. Maybe it *was* just my imagination, she thought. I can't—

No. "There," she said breathlessly, pointing to the side of the screen. "See?"

"I don't know," Bess said. "It's awfully blurry."

For a second it looked as if the "body" teetered precariously at the cliff's edge. Then it plummeted and vanished into darkness.

George drew a long breath. "If it is a body, why didn't TVR notice it before?" she asked.

"I wouldn't have noticed it, either, if I had been really interested in the show," Nancy said. *"Anyone* watching would have missed it, I bet— the rest of the action's so distracting."

"But if it is a body, it's horrible!" Bess said. "What are we going to do about it?"

"What *can* we do?" George asked blankly. "It all happened three years ago, and if no one caught it then—"

"But three years ago—" Bess broke off. "That was Jesse Slade's last concert, and he was never seen after that. What if—"

"No!" George said. "That's impossible, Bess. If Jesse had fallen off a cliff, *someone* would have discovered his body."

"We don't know that for sure," Bess insisted. "Nancy, don't you think it could be Jesse?"

Nancy shook her head. "I think George is right, Bess. There'd have been no way to hide something like that."

"But it all *fits!*" Bess said. "I bet someone murdered him! Nancy, this is your next case, I just know it! You've got to get in touch with TV Rock right away!"

"Whoa!" Nancy said. "I can see it now." She picked up an imaginary phone. " 'Hello, Dan Kennedy? I think I know what happened to Jesse Slade.' They'd never take me seriously, Bess. There's just not enough to go on!"

"Okay. Okay," Bess said, tense. "But if they *did* take you seriously—if they asked you to investigate this—would you do it?"

"I guess so," Nancy replied slowly.

"Then it's all taken care of," Bess said resolutely. "You just leave this to me, Nan."

Nancy couldn't help smiling a little. "Uh, Bess? How exactly are you going to take care of this?"

"Oh, TVR will take me seriously. You'll see,"

Bess answered. "Now, I think the best thing for you and George to do is go home and start packing."

"Bess, I have to hand it to you," Nancy said two days later. "You're very persuasive."

"I'll say," George chimed in. "If anyone had told me I'd be in Los Angeles today, I'd—well, it's hard to believe, anyway."

Twenty-four hours earlier Nancy had gotten a phone call. At first she'd thought it was a joke—that the guy at the other end was some friend of Bess's who'd been asked to play a joke on her. But soon she realized that the caller really was Dan Kennedy. And he really had been calling to find out whether she'd take on this case.

"I have to admit I'm intrigued by the whole thing, Mr. Kennedy," Nancy had said, "but I'm not totally sure there *is* a case to take on."

"Call me Dan," he'd answered. "You may be right, Nancy. But I agree with your friend Bess. Jesse Slade disappears at the same concert where a body mysteriously falls off a cliff—well, it's too much of a coincidence to be a coincidence. And I'm willing to fly you and your friends out here—and put you up at TVR's expense—if you'll agree to take a look around. I hear you're quite a detective. Bess told me about your work with Bent Fender, and I'm impressed."

Bent Fender was a rock group whose lead

singer, Barton Novak, had disappeared just minutes before a concert at Radio City Music Hall. The case had been one of Nancy's most challenging, but she had had more to go on then.

"All right, Dan. I'll give it a try," Nancy said. "But don't you have to get some kind of okay on this?"

"I'll get it okayed later. For now, I'll just put it on my expense account—and if there's a problem, I'll deal with it."

"Well, that's generous of you," Nancy said. "I'll come out with my friends, but I can't make any promises. In fact, I hardly know where to start!"

"Well, let me think about that. I'll try to come up with a few leads by the time you get here," said Dan. "And listen, Nancy—thanks."

That had been a day ago. Nancy had booked a flight for Los Angeles right after talking to Dan. She, Bess, and George had gotten on the plane that morning. They'd arrived just after lunch and rented a car at the L.A. airport. Now they were inching through a four-lane traffic jam toward the TVR studio.

"This is an incredible car," Nancy said. "I've never rented one with a cellular phone *and* super-Sensurround stereo! All this and traffic jams, too? I guess we really *are* in California!"

"If only I'd started my diet when I was supposed to," Bess said wistfully. "I mean, here

15

we're going to be hanging out with rock stars—and I'm five stupid pounds overweight as usual. My one big chance, and I blew it!"

"Bess, you look fine," George said. "How many times have we been over this before?"

"Besides, I bet there aren't going to be a lot of rock stars hanging around TVR," Nancy put in, glancing into the sideview mirror as she carefully changed lanes. "Videos of stars, yes. Stars, no."

For a second Bess looked crestfallen. Then she brightened. "But the TVR veejays are almost like rock stars themselves. I can't wait to meet Dan Kennedy!"

"Whoops!" was all Nancy answered. Honking wildly, a flame-colored Jaguar had abruptly cut in front of the girls' rental car. "This traffic's going to take some getting used to! Let's hope it's not like this all the time."

An hour later Nancy pulled up in front of the three-story limestone building whose address Dan had given her. "Here we are," she said, climbing out and audibly sighing. "Boy, if that's how crowded it gets on the freeways, what's it like to drive on regular roads around here? Well, I guess we'll find out."

She pushed the glass door open into a lobby that was nothing like any other lobby she'd ever seen. It was painted hot pink, and filled with giant plastic palms. In back of the receptionist's desk was a huge screen showing a constant stream of rock videos without the sound. And next to her desk was parked a gleaming silver Porsche with a sign on it that said "Drive Me."

Even the receptionist looked perfectly suited to this place. No older than Nancy, she was wearing a hot pink rubberized dress, lime green stockings printed with tiny neon yellow polka dots, and electric blue high-top leather sneakers. On the black steel desk next to her typewriter was a tiny forest of palm trees just like the ones looming above her. She looked up expectantly as Nancy and her friends approached.

"What's the story with that car?" George asked before Nancy could say a word.

The receptionist smiled. "It belonged to the lead singer of the Slickboys. He gave it to us as a thank-you present when one of their videos went to number one. We didn't know what to do with it, so we just left it out here. Anyway, can I help you?"

"I'm Nancy Drew, and these are my friends Bess Marvin and George Fayne," Nancy told her. "We have an appointment to see Dan Kennedy."

"Have a seat," the receptionist said, gesturing toward a waiting area a few feet away. "I'll give him a call."

She picked up the phone and punched a few numbers. "They're here, Dan," she said. "Oh. Oh, really? Well, okay. I'll send her down."

She hung up and turned back to Nancy. "Dan says you're to see our president, Mr. Thomas, right away," she said. "Your friends can wait here. Dan will be along in a minute to pick them up, and when you're done with Mr. Thomas you can come and meet them."

Uh-oh, Nancy thought. Why do I suddenly feel as if I'm being sent to see the principal? Aloud, though, she just asked, "Which way is Mr. Thomas's office?"

"It's down at the end of the hall. The office with the double doors," said the receptionist.

"See you in a little while," Nancy said, and headed down the hall.

The secretary's desk in front of the office was empty. I guess I'll have to announce myself, Nancy thought.

"Mr. Thomas?" she asked softly, peeking inside the double doors at the man speaking on the phone.

He didn't seem to notice her at first. "Okay. Book them for Friday. I don't care how, and I don't care what it costs—I just want it done!" he said into the receiver. "Now I have to go." Without saying goodbye, he hung up and turned to Nancy. "Yes, I'm Winslow Thomas," he said, "and you must be Nancy Drew." He jumped to his feet to shake her hand. "Please, have a seat."

Except for a huge, bushy ginger-colored beard, Winslow Thomas was the most correct-looking man Nancy had ever seen. He was wearing a navy pinstriped suit, a white shirt, and a navy checked tie. His wingtip oxfords had the burnished shine that could only have come from a professional polishing, and his short, wavy hair looked as though it had been trimmed five minutes ago.

What's he doing at a place like TV Rock? Nancy wondered as she sat down. He should be the head of a bank!

Before she could speculate further, Winslow Thomas cleared his throat. "I'll come right to the point, Nancy," he said. "Dan Kennedy told me this morning that you were coming to investigate the Jesse Slade disappearance." He had a slight southern accent, and his diction was so perfect that it almost sounded affected. "I have to say that I don't think it's a great idea," he continued. "And, frankly, I'm a little irritated at Dan for giving you the go-ahead without checking with me first. If he had, he'd have found out that I think a thing like this is definitely not in TVR's best interests."

"Why not?" Nancy asked, startled.

"A couple of reasons." Winslow Thomas leaned back in his chair. "First of all, the police have officially declared the case closed. It makes us look foolish to open it again with no more substantial evidence than a few seconds of film. Jesse Slade going over a *cliff*? How farfetched can you get?"

"I'll be honest with you, Mr. Thomas," Nancy said. "At first I thought it was a little farfetched myself. But don't you think we should explore any possibility if it could lead us to the right answer?"

19

"Not in this case," Winslow Thomas said. "I'll be honest with you, Nancy. The police don't think anything violent happened to Jesse. They suspect that he had reasons for dropping out of sight—reasons that wouldn't look too good if they became known. I'm afraid I agree with them. From the rumors I've heard—and I hear quite a lot in this business—Jesse Slade wasn't as perfect as his fans believed. But, what's the point of trashing his image now? What's the point of bringing the past to life if all it does is disappoint people?"

"I see your point," Nancy said slowly, "but I don't think that's a good reason for abandoning this case. What if those rumors you've heard *aren't* true? What if there *was* some kind of violence involved? I think it's more important to find out what really happened."

Winslow Thomas paused for a second. "Okay, I'll tell you what," he said briskly. "If you agree to work undercover in the record business—and to work as fast as you can—I'll agree to bankroll you for a reasonable amount of time. But I don't want any publicity. If the answer to this mystery turns out to be unpleasant, I don't want TVR getting a tainted reputation. We're a music station, not a muckraking business. And I don't want you getting my staff all fired up about this. They have jobs to do—and they don't include playing amateur detective."

Was that a dig? Nancy wasn't sure. "You

mentioned my going undercover," she said. "Do you have any suggestions what cover I could use so I could ask lots of questions."

"We use a lot of guest veejays at TVR. A contest-winner who was supposed to be our next guest veejay had to back out at the last minute. Maybe I could tell people that you're here to fill that slot. You could go undercover right here at the station. You'd have access to just about anyone you'd need to talk to."

"That sounds great," Nancy said.

"As long as you really pull your weight," Winslow Thomas added warningly. "As I said, I don't want my staff suspecting anything."

"Don't worry, Mr. Thomas," Nancy said. "I'll work hard. I promise."

"That's settled, then," said Winslow Thomas. "You can start tomorrow. I'll have my secretary call Dan, and he can start showing you the ropes. I've already told him not to let anyone know who you are, by the way. You can go up to his office now. It's one flight up—Room Two Twenty-four."

"Well, I will say one thing, Dan," Nancy said dryly a few minutes later. "Your boss is very efficient. Obviously he had decided to let me work here, but he made me convince him to reopen the case. Even with all of that, he had me in and out of there in five minutes flat."

"You don't have to tell *me* what he's like," Dan

21

said, wincing a little. "We've had our share of run-ins. I'm not too efficient. I'm kind of relaxed, myself."

"Yes, we'd noticed that," George said with a smile.

Nancy had arrived at Dan's office—a tiny cubbyhole of a place filled with wind-up toys, heaps of cassette tapes, and leftover pizza boxes —to find Bess and George chatting with him as if he were an old friend. She could see why. Dan was as easygoing and relaxed as Winslow Thomas had been brisk and formal. He had a mop of curly blond hair and laughing blue eyes, and he was dressed in black jeans, black running shoes, and a Bent Fender T-shirt—"put on in your honor," he'd told her. He was just as funny in person as he was on the air.

"I've got to do a taping before the end of the afternoon," Dan said, "so maybe I'll show you around tomorrow. But are there any questions you have now? I feel kind of responsible for you, since I brought you all the way out here."

"Well, I'd like to take a look at the site of the concert," Nancy said. "And I want to talk to someone on the crew that taped Jesse's last performance."

"Well, you're in luck. I've got a friend who worked on that tape," Dan said. "I'll give you her number."

"Great!" Nancy said. "And maybe you can help me make a list of the people I should talk to.

People who worked with Jesse, I mean. His manager, for instance. I don't even know who that was—"

"Tommy Road." Dan's voice was suddenly clipped and urgent. "Funny you should mention him. You know, since Bess's call I've been thinking a lot about Tommy Road. Did you know he vanished at the same time Jesse did?"

"That's strange," Nancy said.

"*Very* strange." Dan leaned closer. "I'd look into Tommy Road's disappearance closely if I were you," he said in a low voice. "If you want my opinion, Tommy murdered Jesse and hid the body before he disappeared!"

Chapter

Three

YOU SEE, NANCY? I *told* you Jesse Slade was murdered!" Bess said triumphantly.

"Wait a minute," Nancy said. She turned to Dan. "That's quite an accusation, Dan. Where did it come from?"

"Shhh! Don't talk too loudly," Dan murmured. "After my conversation with Mr. Thomas this morning, I don't want him to think I'm taking time away from my job to work on this. Anyway, I don't have any hard evidence or even evidence of any kind.

"But I know that there were bad feelings between Jesse and Tommy Road before they disappeared," he continued. "I was a radio deejay then, and I interviewed Jesse a couple of times. I asked him something about Tommy once, and suddenly Jesse got really angry. I guess that's why I can still remember his exact words. He said, 'Tommy's done nothing to help me—in fact, it's the opposite. Off the record, I'm looking for another manager.' I asked him what he meant, but he wouldn't tell me anything more. Said it was nothing he could prove, and he'd appreciate my forgetting what he said. I did—until now."

"And Tommy Road vanished at the same time Jesse did?" George said slowly, thinking out loud. "I wonder why I never heard about it."

"It got some coverage, but Jesse was such a big star, Tommy's disappearance got buried."

"What was Tommy Road like?" Nancy asked.

"Kind of obnoxious," Dan answered. "I met him at a couple of parties. He was British, and he was always going on about how weak the American music scene was compared to that in England. I always wanted to ask him how he could complain when he was making so much money off an American like Jesse."

"What did he look like?" asked George.

"*Extremely* weird," Dan replied. "He shaved his head way before anyone else did, and he had tattoos on his face."

"Ugh! That sounds a little *too* weird." Bess shuddered.

"Yeah," Dan continued. "Two lizards, one on

each cheek. And he wore a long cape all the time." Dan shot a quick glance at his watch. "Look, I've got to go back to work. You'll be here tomorrow, won't you?"

"I sure will," Nancy answered. "I start work for you guys tomorrow!"

"Well, we can talk more then," Dan said. "Oh! Before I forget—that friend I was telling you about, the one who worked on the concert tape, works near here. She's over on Hollywood Boulevard." He picked up his phone book and handed it to Nancy. "Her name's Cari Levine. Here's her number."

Nancy jotted it down. "Can I use your phone to call her?" she asked.

"Be my guest. Okay, I'm out of here. See you tomorrow," Dan said and vanished out the door.

Nancy picked up the phone and began dialing the number Dan had given her. Bess sighed. "What a great guy."

"Really," George agreed. "Nan, can't you figure out some way to get us a job here, too?"

"Oh, I'll be keeping you busy enough. Hello, is this Cari Levine? My name is Nancy Drew. Dan Kennedy gave me your name. I'm doing some research on Jesse Slade." Nancy couldn't mention the fact that she was a private investigator. She didn't want to blow her cover. "I know this is short notice," she went on, "but I was wondering if you could spare a moment to talk to me and my friends about the night of his last concert."

"No problem," Cari said warmly. "Come right over."

"Hey! There's Melrose Avenue," Bess said as they drove toward Cari's office. "There are supposed to be incredible shops all along there. You know, I've been *needing* a little bit of L.A. to take back home with me. Like that stuff there." She pointed at a store window filled with peach-colored leather clothes being worn by mannequins turned upside-down. "Nancy, don't you think we could—"

"Not now," Nancy said firmly. "You'll get a chance to shop, I promise. But not now."

Cari Levine's office, which was on the ninth floor of a black glass skyscraper, was even messier than Dan's. Cans of film were everywhere, and snipped-off bits of tape littered the floor. The posters taped to the walls had all come unstuck on at least one corner.

Cari herself looked bright and energetic. She was wearing a scarlet jumpsuit with matching ankle boots, and from elbow to wrist her arms were lined with a mass of jangling silver bracelets.

"Sorry about the mess," Cari said. "I keep meaning to clean it up, but somehow every day goes by without my touching a thing. So, enough of my apologies. What can I do for you?"

Nancy explained. "We were wondering if

you'd noticed anything out of the ordinary that night," she said, finishing up.

"I was just a lowly assistant back then," Cari said. "I never actually talked to Jesse, but even I couldn't help notice that he was kind of edgy. He kept yelling at people while we were setting up—and that was the kind of thing that never happened with Jesse. Normally he went out of his way to be nice to camera crews and roadies and people like that."

"Did he say anything that seemed strange to you?" Nancy pressed.

"Well, it *was* three years ago...." Cari thought for a minute. "And the main thing we were all paying attention to was the weather."

"The weather?" George repeated.

"Yes. We were all afraid it was going to rain. The sky looked incredibly dark and threatening, and you could hear thunder in the distance. As a matter of fact, there *was* a big storm right after the concert ended. Perfect timing! If the concert had been the next day, the whole stage would have had to have been rebuilt—the rain made half the cliff collapse."

Nancy looked up, suddenly alert. "Does that happen often?" she asked.

"Well, we do have a big problem with the coast eroding out here," Cari answered. "I'm sure you've heard about all the big beach houses on Malibu that have wound up in the ocean because the shoreline erodes so badly."

Nancy didn't answer for a second. "The timing . . ." she finally said. Bess, George, and Cari all stared at her, but Nancy didn't notice. "It's another case of the timing being too good," she said slowly. "Jesse disappears . . . the cliff he was performing on crumbles . . . and a body that may have fallen off the cliff is never found."

"You're not saying someone *made* the cliff collapse, are you?" George asked. "Nancy, that was obviously just—just nature! It can't have anything to do with Jesse's disappearance!"

"Oh, I'm not saying anyone engineered the collapse," Nancy said quickly. "All I mean is that the body might have been buried under the cliff when it collapsed. That might account for no one's discovering it!"

Nancy jumped to her feet. "Well, I wanted to see the site of the concert anyway," she said. "And there's no time like the present. Let's head out to the beach and take a look. It's not much of a lead, but it might tell us something. Can you give me directions to the site, Cari?"

"Sure," Cari said. "It's about an hour north of here. Now, if I can just find a map in all this mess . . . Forget it; I'll just tag along and show you."

"I can't believe how beautiful this is," Bess said half an hour later. "It looks like something from a movie!"

29

"From many movies," Cari answered. "This shot must be in hundreds of them."

The four girls were standing at the edge of a cliff that jutted out into the churning, white-capped ocean. Below them waves pounded relentlessly against glistening black rocks, and the air was filled with the cry of sea gulls.

"Where are the surfers?" Bess asked. She sounded disappointed. "This place is totally deserted."

"Well, look at the water!" George said. "No one could surf or swim here. It's much too wild, and those rocks would be horrible to crash into." Suddenly she shivered. "I feel sorry for Jesse if he did fall off this cliff. I don't see any way he could have survived."

"You're right," Nancy said. "It would have been almost impossible to investigate, too, especially once the cliff had collapsed.

"Let's see. The band must have been over there." Nancy gestured to a point about thirty feet away. "Right?" Cari nodded.

"And the taping crew was right where we're standing now," Cari added. "That means that the body I saw falling had to have been standing over there."

There was a spot at the edge of the cliff that overhung a huge boulder. Bess eyed it nervously.

"You're not planning to investigate *that*, I hope," she said. "Because if you are, I have to tell you I'd rather be shopping."

"Well, it would be nice to get a closer look," Nancy said. "I wonder what's the best way to get down to the beach."

Cari shrugged. "That, I don't know."

Nancy and Cari walked over to the spot and stared down at the shore.

"It's kind of windy, you two," Bess said fretfully. "Get back a little, will you?"

Cari inched back one foot, but Nancy kept looking down. "I guess I was expecting to *see* a collapsed cliff," she mused. "But, of course, that doesn't make any sense. Three years of tides moving in and out would smooth over the spot, wouldn't they? So there'd be no trace of a body now or of the rubble."

Bess's voice was edgy. "Nancy, Cari, you *know* I hate heights! Let's get out of here and go back and check into the hotel. I'm starving!"

"In one second," Nancy promised. "I'm just trying to fix this scene in my—"

Then she gasped. Under her heels, the cliff was starting to crumble, and the momentum shot her forward.

Instinctively Nancy threw herself back. Her arms flailed the air wildly—helplessly.

Cari made a lunge for her, but came up with nothing but a handful of air.

Nancy's frantic backpedaling only made things worse. Before she could draw a breath to scream, she was sliding down the rocky face to the treacherous boulders below.

31

Chapter

Four

NANCY SLID with her arms stretched above her head, grasping for any handhold. She held her breath, waiting for the terrible moment when she'd smash onto the rocks below.

Then a third of the way down, her shirt shredded and her back skinned, Nancy sped past a small bush rooted precariously in the rock. She opened her hand and clawed at it. Her fall was stopped, but the impact was terrible. Nancy hung, dangling by one arm, her shoulder wrenched and aching.

But she was alive!

She eased her toes down onto a narrow outcropping of rock—just a yard wide—jutting out from the cliff. Below her, the sea licked at the rocks as hungrily as ever.

Nancy lay there trembling. Every inch of her body was throbbing with pain, but she knew nothing was broken. Her shoulder was not dislocated. She ran a hand across her eyes and glanced back up at the cliff top. The others were staring down at her, ashen faced.

"H-hi," Nancy stuttered.

There were tears in Bess's eyes. She opened her mouth to return Nancy's greeting, but no sound came out.

"Don't move," George called. "I'll be right down to help you."

"No, I'm okay!" Nancy called back. "Just a little sore. And embarrassed," she added. "I can climb up myself."

Now that she looked, she noticed that the cliff was *covered* with scraggly bushes. Nancy slid along to the end of the ledge and pulled gingerly on the nearest one. It didn't move. She gave it a harder tug. The bush certainly seemed well rooted.

"I can use these bushes to pull myself up," she called up to the girls. "But keep an eye on me."

"We will," Bess said fervently as Nancy edged herself off the ledge and began her ascent.

"No, Ned, I'm okay. Really!" Nancy insisted. "A little bit scraped up, that's all." She felt the pain shoot down her arm when she eased her shoulder back and tried not to groan audibly. "It's sweet of you to want to fly out here, but I'm just not going to let you. Not with that big paper to finish . . ."

It was nine at night, and Nancy had just put in a good-night call to Ned at college. She still couldn't believe her good luck. She'd made it back up the cliff with very little trouble. Her knees and elbows were rubbed raw from the climb—but she would be okay soon.

"The fall did tell me something," she said to Ned. "It's entirely possible that whoever fell in that tape slid down just the way I did—because of the cliff's collapsing."

"So there might not have been any kind of 'foul play' involved?" Ned asked.

"Exactly. But I don't know what it all proves. It's just something to file away."

"Well, keep me filed away somewhere, too," Ned said. "I hate having you so far away."

"Me, too." Nancy sighed. "I'd better hang up. I've got a lot going on tomorrow—first day on the job, you know. I love you."

"I love you, too, Nancy. Call me again as soon as you can."

"Nancy, hi! You're right on time!"

Nancy turned to see Dan Kennedy striding toward her. "I'm starting to get the hang of driving around here," she said. "You just leave an hour earlier than you think you need to."

"That's about it," Dan said. "What have you done with Bess and George?"

Nancy hid a smile. Her friends would be delighted to hear that he'd asked about them. "They're working," she said. "I gave them their assignments last night. Before we left for L.A., I called Jesse's estate to find out who his accountants were. It's a firm called Lawrence Associates, and Bess is over there now trying to get permission to go through Jesse's financial records. George is at the library looking at old newspaper clippings of that last concert. Something might turn up—you never know."

"Well, tell them hi for me. Now, I'll take you around and introduce you to the people you'll be working with this week." Dan lowered his voice. "I've told them you're a guest veejay, even the receptionist."

Speaking normally again, he took Nancy by the shoulders and piloted her down the hall. "Let's go find out what a rock TV station looks like," he said.

"Here's the control room," he said, stopping beside one door. "There are three directors inside—the director, the associate director, and the technical director. The technical director's responsible for making sure the right tape's put on when it's time to show a video." Nancy pulled the door open a crack and peered in to see a man and two women sitting at a paneled board covered with what looked like millions of buttons.

35

On the wall in front of them were four television screens, each showing the set from a different angle. She eased the door closed again.

"And here's the sound room," Dan continued, indicating a room with a sliding glass door adjacent to the control room. "It's just what it sounds like—the technician here monitors the show's decibel level."

Dan stuck his head into the sound room and tapped the shoulder of a man wearing headphones. "Wake up, Ken! This is Nancy Drew," he said after the technician had turned around. "She's our new guest veejay. She'll be—"

"I have a lot of work to do," Ken said flatly, interrupting. "I'll talk to you later." And he turned his back on them.

For a second Dan looked bewildered. "Well, *he's* sure got something on his mind," he said. "Maybe one of the higher-ups has been giving him trouble."

They peeked into the makeup room, the editing room, and the preview room—a soundproof chamber where tapes could be played at all different sound levels to make sure the sound was undistorted. A bright red and white electric guitar was propped up against one wall of the sound room. "What's that guitar for?" Nancy asked.

"Oh, that! We had a demo band practicing in here a couple of days ago, and—if you can believe it—they forgot that. I don't think they're going to get far in this business."

Dan introduced Nancy to several more people. She couldn't understand it, but no one she met was very friendly—and a couple of people were even downright rude. As she and Dan continued on, Dan looked more and more confused.

"They don't know who you really are, do they?" he muttered.

"I don't see how they could!" Nancy whispered back. "And even if they did, why would they be *angry* at me?"

"Beats me," said Dan. "But something's going on, that's for sure. Here's the studio. They're taping now, so we'll just slip in the back door. Be very quiet. This is where it all happens."

The studio was an enormous room three stories high—the height of the whole building. The first thing Nancy noticed was that it was freezing in there. "It's so hot under all those lights that the rest of the room has to be kept cold so the veejays won't get too sweaty," Dan whispered.

Nancy looked up at the ceiling. It was hung with massive lights, each burning down onto the set.

"Why do they need three cameras?" she whispered to Dan, staring at the set.

"One's for the center, one's for closeups, and one's for the guest chair," he answered.

The center chair was where the veejay sat. One

was sitting there then in front of a large screen that was pulsing with color and weird shapes.

"What does he do when the video's on?" Nancy asked.

"Anything he wants—for as long as the video lasts. They run the tape in from the control room. Well, I've got just one more person to introduce you to, and that's Renee Stanley. I think she's in the dressing room. She's the veejay who'll be your boss this week."

"I've seen her on TV. She's great," said Nancy as they headed down the hall again. "But I thought my boss was going to be you."

"I wish I could be." Dan sounded genuinely regretful. "But all this Jesse Slade–week stuff's going to keep me too busy. I'll do everything I can to help you, though."

"Okay," Nancy said. She was trying to fight down the rush of nervousness that was rising in her stomach. I know this is just an undercover job, she thought. But if everyone's got a grudge against me, I'm going to need an ally. Maybe Renee will—

But one look at Renee Stanley and Nancy knew *she* wasn't going to be on her side.

The dressing room door was open. Three of the walls were lined with signed photos of rock stars, and the fourth was hung ceiling to floor with one huge mirror. Renee was sitting and brushing her hair, staring fixedly at her reflection when they walked into her office. She didn't stop brushing

—didn't even turn around—as Dan introduced Nancy. Then, very deliberately, she put her brush down and swiveled her chair around to face Nancy.

She was even prettier in person than on TV. She was wearing zebra-print tights and a low-cut sleeveless black T-shirt with a loose-fitting leather belt riding down on her hips. Tousled blond ringlets framed her heart-shaped face. Her eyes were a startlingly deep blue—almost violet—with lashes so long they cast shadows on her cheeks.

But there was nothing pretty about her expression, or about the silence that hung in the air as she stared first at Nancy and then at Dan.

Dan cleared his throat nervously. "I don't know whether you have time to talk to Nancy before you go on——" he began.

"Not really," Renee interrupted. "But I guess I don't have much of a choice, do I?" She glanced briefly at Nancy and picked up a hand mirror. "Well, you might as well sit down, Nancy," she said in a bored monotone. "Got a pad? I want you to take notes."

"Nancy, you look awful!" George said anxiously as Nancy walked slowly across the lobby of TVR. "I didn't find out much at the library—but I guess that had better wait. How was your day?"

Nancy tried to smile. "Not the greatest. I thought four-thirty would never come. If this is the glamorous world of music television, you can have it." Wearily she ran a hand across her face. "Where's the car?"

George had dropped Nancy off that morning. Since Bess had been headed in a different direction, she took a taxi. "It's over there," George said, pointing across the street. "Do you want to go back to the hotel? You look as though you could use a rest."

"Not yet," answered Nancy. "We're going to see someone. I did get one lead today. Do you have the keys, George? I'd like to drive. Okay?"

"I don't know what I've done, but everyone at TVR is mad at me," she said as she pulled the car onto the freeway and headed toward the suburbs. "They must have been told something really horrible about me. But what? And by whom, I keep asking myself.

"Renee Stanley's *really* got it in for me," she continued. "All I did today was clerical stuff—that and errands. Renee treated me like a secretary. She sent me out to get her lunch. She made me type letters for her—thank-you notes for some birthday presents. She made me alphabetize some files. I wouldn't have minded—I mean, it's nice to help out—but she didn't say a civil word to me the whole day!"

"You should tell Mr. Thomas," George said indignantly.

"Oh, I can't do that," said Nancy. "I'm sure it would get out if I did, and then people would be angry at me for tattling. I'll just have to tough it out. But somehow I don't think I'll be learning a lot about the music business or meeting the right people to ask my questions."

"Say, where are we going?" asked George. "You said something about a lead?"

Nancy brightened. "Yes. I did get a chance to talk to Dan in the afternoon—he said to say hi to you, by the way—and he suggested that I talk to Vint Wylie. He was Jesse's bass player, and Dan thinks Vint probably knew Jesse as well as anyone in the business. So I made an appointment with him. He lives in a suburb called North Claibourne—we have two more exits to go."

"What's Vint Wylie doing now?" asked George.

"I don't know. Maybe he's playing in another band," Nancy answered. "Whatever he's doing, I hope he's nicer to me than the people at TVR," she added with a sigh.

They reached the exit and drove for a couple of miles before Nancy reached the right neighborhood. "This is North Claibourne. How gorgeous!" she exclaimed. "Look at all those beautiful gardens!"

They *were* beautiful. Every yard was lushly planted, every lawn an emerald rectangle. Flowering trees were everywhere, and their colors were nothing like those near Nancy's home—flaming reds, corals, and yellows. The houses were no less beautiful. Most of them were one story high, and most looked vaguely Spanish, with red-tiled roofs and stucco walls.

"It all looks sort of tropical," George said. "But so respectable, too. I can hardly believe a bass player would live around here. But I guess he has to live somewhere. Are we almost there, Nan?"

"*Right* there. Right now," answered Nancy as she looked at the address Dan had given her. "Wow! Vint Wylie's certainly done well for himself!"

At the end of a long, winding, flower-edged driveway, behind impressive wrought-iron gates, was a sprawling Tudor mansion—the only two-story house on the block.

The gates were open. "He's expecting us," Nancy said, turning carefully into the driveway and switching off the ignition. "He sounded very nice on the phone—said to come over."

There was no answer when she rang the bell. Nancy stood on tiptoe to peer in through the little lead-paned window in the door. All she could see was a dark, deserted-looking interior. There was no trace of anyone inside.

Gently Nancy tried the door. It was unlocked.

She and George eyed each other questioningly. "Should we go in?" George whispered.

"I don't know," Nancy whispered back. "Wait, why are we whispering?" she said in full voice. "Of course we should go in. He's expecting us. Maybe he's on the phone or something."

But no one was inside the dark, cavernous house with its carpets so thick the girls' steps were completely muffled. And the phone in the hall was off the hook.

Nancy stepped into the gleaming kitchen, which looked big enough to serve an entire restaurant. Through the kitchen window she could see the bright turquoise water of a swimming pool. "He must be out in back," she said, walking resolutely toward the kitchen's french doors.

She stepped outside—and gasped.

Sunlight was dancing on the little ripples in the pool, and a gentle breeze stirred the leaves of the trees overhanging the yard. It was a picture-perfect setting—except for one thing.

A man's body was lying facedown next to the pool!

Chapter

Five

"Oh, no!" Nancy cried.

As George looked on, horrified, she raced up to the motionless figure sprawled on the tiles and grabbed his shoulder. "Call an ambulance!" she ordered George. "There's a cordless phone on that table over there!" George dashed over to it.

Then the man stirred a little, groaned, and lifted his head. Now Nancy could see that he was very handsome, with a bronzed, appealingly craggy face. But he looked completely stunned.

His dazed eyes met Nancy's. "Wha—" he began.

"Mr. Wylie?" Nancy asked. He nodded. "I'm

44

Nancy Drew. It's all right. We're getting help," she reassured him. "You just take it easy."

"But I—" Vint Wylie groaned again and rolled over onto his back, raising himself up on his elbows.

Nancy patted his shoulder. "You'd better not move too much—just in case," she said. "Not until the ambulance gets here."

"But I'm okay," Vint Wylie said thickly. George had been dialing, but she stopped and stared at him. He gave an enormous yawn. "Sorry. I was just, uh, meditating."

"Meditating! You *look* as if you were—" George exclaimed. Nancy cut her off quickly. She knew George was about to say "asleep." And she was sure George was right. But there was no point in embarrassing Vint Wylie unnecessarily —he would talk more freely if he didn't feel self-conscious.

"Sorry if we startled you," she said. "We—well, obviously we thought there was something the matter. I guess I jumped to conclusions."

"It's sure lucky I hadn't reached the ambulance company yet," George said, a shade tartly. "It would have been embarrassing to have them get here and find out Mr. Wylie was okay after all."

"Call me Vint, you two. 'Mr. Wylie' sounds too weird. I don't think anyone's ever called me that before." He brushed the dark-brown hair out of his eyes and yawned once. He had meditated himself right into a deep sleep. Suddenly he grinned at Nancy, a slow, infectious grin.

"Great intro!" he said. "Shall we start all over?"

Nancy smiled back. "Sounds good," she replied. "Vint, this is my friend George Fayne. She's helping me on my—uh—research."

Vint gestured toward some teak chairs, and the three of them sat down while Nancy explained why they'd come. "Dan Kennedy said you knew the most about Jesse," she finished. "You two were pretty close?"

"Sort of." Vint bit his lip. "Jesse wasn't— wasn't that easy to get to know, really. He was probably the most private person I've ever known."

"No family?" Nancy asked. "No close friends?"

Vint looked away. He cleared his throat a couple of times, then sighed. "No. He did have a girlfriend," he said slowly. He drummed his fingers nervously on his knee. "I—I don't know about his family, though."

Why does he seem so tense? Nancy wondered. I'm not asking him anything to make him nervous. Aloud, she just said, "Do you know his girlfriend's name? Maybe I should talk to her."

"I—I don't know what her name was," Vint said quickly. "I can find out for you, though."

"That would be great. What about your band's

manager, Tommy Road? Did you know him well?" asked Nancy.

"That creep? I knew much too much about him," said Vint. He put his hands behind his head and stretched his legs out in front of him. In this elegant garden, his faded jeans and cowboy boots seemed out of place. "How much time have you got?" Suddenly he looked much more relaxed.

"Well, Dan Kennedy mentioned something about Jesse's wanting to fire Tommy Road. Had you heard anything about that?" Nancy asked.

"Jesse wanted to *fire* him?" Vint sounded astonished. "I can't believe it! He would never hear a word against him. I mean, *we* all knew what a loser Tommy was, but Jesse always refused to consider switching managers."

He scratched his chin thoughtfully. "Though there was some problem with money. Jesse was always short."

"Short of *money?*" George asked. "How could that happen? I mean, his records sold in the millions."

"I know. But it's true," Vint said. "He used to talk a lot about it. He paid me and everyone else who worked for him on time, but he was always grumbling about how he didn't have enough. That could be what finally came between him and Tommy. But as I said, I didn't know anything was up between them.

"I can tell you one person who might be able to

help you, though," he said, straightening up in his chair. "His name's Martin Rosenay. He lives out in Chelmsford—that's a town about twenty miles east of here. He really gets around in the music business—he's a dealer in rock memorabilia. And I hear he's done pretty well selling stuff related to Jesse. He probably has tons of photos, letters, and junk."

Vint stood up abruptly. "I guess I haven't been much help," he said. "I'm sorry. But I'm sure this guy Rosenay will be better."

It was definitely a dismissal. Nancy and George stood up, too. "Thanks, Vint," Nancy said. "Actually, you've been very helpful." Not *that* helpful, really, she said to herself. "Can I call you if I have any more questions?" she added.

"Sure! Any time!" Vint sounded a little too enthusiastic.

"Oh, there is one thing I forgot to ask," Nancy said. "What are you doing now? For a living, I mean?"

Now Vint looked troubled. "I'm in another band," he said. "You've probably heard of them. The Crisp."

"The Crisp! But they're—"

"Doing incredibly well," Vint finished for her. "It's true. But I'd trade it all in just to be able to play with Jesse again."

And this time Nancy was sure he was telling the truth.

"Well, what did you think?" George asked, when they were safely back in the car again.

"There's something going on," Nancy said, "but I'm not sure what. Did you notice it, too?"

"How could I miss it? When you asked him about Jesse's friends and girlfriend, he just about shriveled up."

"Yes, that's it," Nancy agreed. "But I was afraid that if I pressed him harder, he'd clam up altogether. I'll try again later."

She glanced at her watch. "It's almost supper-time. Let's go back to the hotel and meet Bess and hear how her day went."

The "hotel" where the three girls were staying was actually a group of small bungalows, each with its own kitchen and garage. "Boy, am I exhausted," Nancy said as she parked the car in their garage. "I feel so dirty, too. All I want to do tonight is—"

"Nancy!" Bess was at Nancy's elbow before Nancy was out of the car. "George! You're back! I've been waiting for you guys forever!"

She practically dragged Nancy out. "I've found out something *very interesting* about Jesse Slade," she said breathlessly. "A huge amount of his money is missing—and I'm sure Tommy Road was embezzling it!"

Chapter

Six

Nancy STOPPED on the path leading into the bungalow and stared at Bess. "We were just *talking* to someone who thought Jesse might have been having money problems," she said. "What did you find out?" All of a sudden she didn't feel so tired.

"Well, come in and sit down and I'll tell you," Bess said. "I just made some iced tea."

Her face was pink with excitement—and pride. "Now, are you ready?" she asked. "You're not going to believe I figured this all out on my own!"

Bess took a big swig of iced tea. "Well, I got to Mr. Lawrence's—the accountant's—office," she began. "It's a big, dark, and gloomy-looking place that looks like a men's club or something. I was a little scared, but I acted official and asked a secretary to see a computer printout of the general ledger Jesse's manager had kept—just the way you rehearsed me, Nan. I was told I could read it in this little conference room right next door to Lawrence's office. So I took this huge stack of computer paper and went in there and started looking through all the payments Tommy Road ever made while he was Jesse's manager.

"Most of it I could figure out pretty well," Bess continued, "but there were these huge payments to something called Bailey Promotional. That's where I started to get confused—because there were also huge payments to a public-relations place called Swang and Davis, and both companies were listed in the promotional category in the ledger. And public relations and promotion are pretty much the same thing, aren't they? Besides, the amount being paid to Bailey Promotional was really huge—I mean, hundreds of thousands of dollars. I don't know that much about this kind of thing, but I didn't see how *any* PR place could charge that much!

"*So.* I decided to call them up and just *ask* them about Tommy Road and Jesse. And guess what!" Bess was practically bouncing in her seat. "There was no Bailey Promotional in the directory! Isn't that fantastic?"

"But they could be unlisted," George objected.

"Oh, no. See, this is where I *really* got smart. I called the California Secretary of State's office. They have a list of all the businesses incorporated in the state. So I asked if they had a listing for a corporation called Bailey Promotional. And they did. It didn't have an address—just a post office box number. And it had been incorporated by a guy named S. Thomas *R-H-O-D-E."*

"Tommy Road! Bess, that's great!" said Nancy. "He was sending Jesse's money to a corporation he'd set up! But how could the accountant have missed that?"

"Well, I finally worked up the guts to talk to Mr. Lawrence," said Bess. "He said that it wasn't his business to question payments that Jesse's manager had authorized. He just paid them. He also said there are lots of different kinds of promotional expenses. So what do you think?"

"I think you did a wonderful job," Nancy said sincerely, and George nodded her agreement. "I don't see how there's any other way to figure this—Tommy Road must have been embezzling, and Jesse must have found out. At last, a real lead! Now we have a motive—a reason someone would have wanted Jesse out of the way."

Then Nancy's face fell. "Oh. But it's going to have to wait," she said in a disappointed voice. "Renee told me that tomorrow's going to be completely crazy. She said I'd really have to buckle down—as if I haven't already been."

"How'd your day go, anyway?" Bess asked. "I forgot to ask."

"Don't ask," Nancy and George said in unison. Nancy grinned. "At least not until after supper," she said. "Let's go find a good Mexican place. Los Angeles is supposed to have millions of them."

"Perfect," Bess replied. "I was so excited about this embezzling thing that I didn't even notice how hungry I was—if you can believe that."

Without meaning to, Nancy and George spoke in unison again. "I can't," they both said.

"Nancy, why did you ever let me eat so much? I feel like a gorged boa constrictor!" Bess groaned theatrically as they walked back into the bunga-low a couple of hours later.

Nancy laughed. "Bess, I refuse all responsibili-ty. No one was forcing you to order that food, you know."

"I know." Bess sighed. "But I've got to blame *somebody.* Do you guys want to see if there's anything good on TV?"

"Not tonight," Nancy said. "I need a good night's sleep. I'm getting up at six tomorrow so I can go in to TVR early. I even arranged for a wake-up call."

"How? By telepathy?" George asked. "I've been with you ever since you left the office, and I haven't seen you go *near* a phone."

"I made the call from TVR," Nancy said, flushing a little. "I wanted to make sure Renee knew I was really trying hard."

Bess—who had heard the whole story of Nancy's day during dinner—leaned over and gave her a hug. "You'll show that Renee," she said comfortingly. "You just wait until tomorrow. She won't know what hit her."

Songbirds were going full-blast outside as the sun streamed in across Nancy's bed and landed directly in her face. Groggily she rolled over and looked at her watch. Then she sat bolt upright in bed.

The hotel management was supposed to wake her at six o'clock. Now it was after eight!

"They must have forgotten about me!" she gasped, throwing the covers back and jumping out of bed. "Oh, I'm going to be so late!"

A tousled-looking Bess peered in, rubbing her eyes. "You're still here?" she said, yawning.

"I sure am," Nancy said grimly, "and the second I'm dressed, I'm calling the hotel desk to find out what happened."

She hurried into a pair of acid-washed jeans and an oversize sleeveless orange shirt. Then she picked up the phone and punched the number of the bell desk.

"This is Nancy Drew. I asked to be woken at six," she said angrily when the clerk answered. "Why didn't it happen?"

"But, Ms. Drew, what about your note?" The woman at the other end sounded astonished.

"What note?"

"Well, I just got on duty, but there's a note on the desk canceling your wake-up call. It's signed with your name. I—I guess the clerk just assumed you had dropped it off. I mean, why wouldn't he?" The clerk sounded completely at sea. "Ms. Drew," she said, "there's obviously been some kind of mix-up. I'm so sorry—I don't know what to say."

"Oh, don't worry," Nancy heard herself answering. "It's not your fault, and anyway, it doesn't matter too much."

And that's really true, she told herself. I have to remember that my job at TVR isn't a real job. But *someone* left that note. Someone's trying to make me look bad at TVR. And I have a very good idea who it is. But I'm not going to give her the satisfaction of thinking she's getting to me.

"Where have you been, Nancy?" Renee asked an hour later. "I thought I told you this was going to be a big day."

Renee sounded offhand, but there was an undercurrent of anger in her voice. Nancy did her best to ignore it. She'd decided on her way over that the most professional way to handle this would be to act as though it had never happened. Renee had probably sent that note—

at least, Nancy couldn't think of anyone else at TVR who would have done such a thing—but on the off-chance that she hadn't, it would definitely be wiser not to confront her.

"I'm very sorry, Renee" was all Nancy said. "What would you like me to do first?"

"Well, I know you don't have any experience working with entertainers," Renee said, "but you're about to get some. A stand-up comic named Bonzo Bob is coming in today. He's been doing the comedy clubs recently, and I'd like you to talk to him to see if you think there's any way you can use him on your show. See what you think, anyway."

"Oh, that sounds like fun!" Nancy said, trying to hide her sarcasm. She could hardly believe her luck. She was supposed to be talking to people in the music business about Jesse, and she had to interview a *comic*.

It didn't take long for Nancy to realize that Bonzo Bob was not going to be on TVR. Nancy couldn't remember ever seeing anyone who made her feel less like laughing. And she'd never seen anyone with so little talent act so temperamental.

Bonzo Bob came bouncing into the little office where Renee had set Nancy up and shouted, "All right! Let's party! I'm a party dude!"

Oh, no, Nancy thought. What is he *wearing?*

Yellow-checked bicycle shorts, wingtip shoes

with gartered black socks, a red sleeveless tank top, and a white beret with a graduation-cap tassel were what Bonzo Bob obviously thought would make people remember him. But he doesn't look funny, Nancy thought—just dumb. Well, maybe he was nicer than he looked.

"I'm Nancy Drew," Nancy said, smiling. "I'm the guest veejay for this week. It's great to meet you, Bonzo—uh, I mean Bob."

For a long minute Bonzo Bob stared goggle-eyed at her. Then he opened his mouth and bellowed, *"Whaaaaat?* So TVR doesn't think I'm good enough for a *real* staff person to interview me, is that right? They think it's okay to send a lousy *guest?* Well, I've got news for you, Miss so-called veejay. Bonzo Bob is worth a lot more than that! Do you know how many people come to see my act at Attention Talent? A lot more than come to see *you!"*

Stay poised, Nancy told herself. You never have to see him again. "Please, won't you sit down?" she asked in as composed a voice as she could manage. "I promise to be as—as 'real' as I can."

"Sure you do," he answered bitterly. Nancy still couldn't tell if he was genuinely angry or if he thought he was being funny. "I believe that like I believe politicians tell the truth. And speaking of politics . . ."

It was all downhill from there. By lunchtime

Nancy's ears hurt from being screamed at, and she could count on one finger the number of jokes that had made her even smile. Bonzo Bob had spent the time alternating between insulting her lowly status at TVR and spewing out the worst humor she had ever heard. When he finally stormed out—again, without making it clear whether or not he was kidding—Nancy felt limp with relief.

"Well, I guess he's not right for us," Renee said briefly when Nancy described her morning's work. "Look, whip down to the commissary and get some lunch to go. I've got another job for you."

Not a word of thanks for all her wasted effort! Nancy was fuming as she walked down the hall toward the commissary.

When she came back with her turkey sandwich, she encountered Renee bent over a street guide. "See this intersection?" she said, pointing to a map. "There's a great bargain basement there called Kendall's. All the kids in the Valley use it—and today they're having a massive sale. I want you to head over there and find out what the scene's like. Take notes, buy a few things if they look interesting—TVR will reimburse you. We're thinking of doing a fashion segment."

Nancy tried to remain cheerful, but it was hard. All this running around wasn't answering any of her questions. It looked as though being undercover was going to be more of a hindrance than a help.

"The scene" at Kendall's turned out to be a huge store, all on one level, filled with long tables. All of them were heaped with jumbled piles of ultrafashionable clothes. The aisles were jammed with girls who were snatching clothes off the tables and trying them on wherever they happened to be.

Nancy took a deep breath and waded in. There was a table of tops in front of her. Curious, she reached out to pick up a leopard-print vest with skull-and-crossbones buttons, but just as she did, a lightning-quick hand snaked in from behind her and grabbed the vest. "I saw it first!" a girl squealed.

Too bad Bess isn't here, Nancy thought. *She'd* actually enjoy this madhouse!

It was almost four o'clock when Nancy finally got back to TVR. Tired but satisfied, she walked up to Renee's cubicle. In her hand was a shopping bag stuffed with clothes. She'd had to wait in line forty-five minutes to pay for them, but it was worth it. The clothes were some of the weirdest she'd ever seen, and she had decided that Kendall's would be a great place to feature on TVR.

Renee was in her office, bent over a pile of

fan mail. "Well, it's really a madhouse there, but I think you could get some—" Nancy started.

She never finished. "Where on earth have you been?" Renee shrieked. "You go on the air in five minutes!"

Chapter

Seven

NANCY DROPPED THE BAG of clothes to the floor. "What do you mean?" she said.

Renee was already propelling her down the hall in the direction of the studio. "I told you you'd be doing a live guest-veejay appearance at four!" she cried. "You're interviewing Carla Tarleton!"

"Carla Tarleton?"

"Yes. She's the lead singer for the Temple of Doom."

Nancy's heart sank. The Temple of Doom was a heavy-metal group whom she'd only seen on TVR once or twice. Nancy felt as if she were trapped in a nightmare. "I'm sorry, Renee, but you didn't mention anything about this!" Nancy panted as they raced along.

"I most certainly did tell you about it," Renee snapped. "Yesterday, just before you left. I remember it clearly."

Quickly Nancy reviewed the events of the day before. She was absolutely sure Renee hadn't said anything. This had to be another way she was trying to sabotage Nancy's work at TVR.

But I'm not going to give her that chance, Nancy vowed. I'll make good on this if it kills me!

"Well, there must have been some mix-up," she said in as calm a voice as she could manage. "Just fill me in on what I need to do, and I'll try the best I can not to mess up."

"It's too late to fill you in," Renee scolded her. "Just keep looking at the camera. Someone will cue you when they're about to switch over to a video. Here we are. No time to make you up— they'll have to do it during the first commercial."

They were at the studio door now. Renee pushed it open.

"Where was she?" someone hissed as Nancy and Renee rushed toward the set. "I'll explain later," Renee shot back over her shoulder. "Is Carla here?"

"Yes. I'm her agent," a dark-haired young woman answered. "We wanted some time for Carla to talk to the veejay first. It's really not fair to make a star go on without any warm-up, you know!"

To Nancy's intense relief, Renee didn't blame her for being late. All her energy seemed concentrated on making sure Nancy got on the air. "Sorry. A mix-up," Renee told the agent. "Can't do anything about it now. Okay, Nancy. Here's your chair."

She pushed Nancy into the anchor's seat in front of the camera. "Good luck."

Nancy's heart was pounding, and her hands were clammy. Face the camera, she told herself. And smile!

She looked up and stared into the camera. It was like staring into space. All she could see was the camera—everything else was black. Above her, the floodlights were beating down, but Nancy wasn't even conscious of how hot it was. Every nerve was concentrated on making this work.

A technician to the side of the camera waved to get Nancy's attention. He held up ten fingers— ten seconds to go. Nine. Eight. Seven. Six. Nancy felt as if she had a metal band being pulled tight across her chest. Five. Four. Three. I can't do this! she thought wildly. Two. One. She was on.

Nancy smiled into the blackness and was startled by the sound of her own voice. "Hello. I'm Nancy Drew, your guest veejay," she began, "and I'm brand-new at this. You have to bear with me for a little while because I'm so nervous I can hardly breathe, much less speak." There was a stifled laugh off-camera.

Now Carla Tarleton was slipping into the seat next to Nancy's. Nancy could hear her breathing fast and knew Carla was nervous, too. That realization made Nancy feel much calmer.

"Today we're going to be talking to Carla Tarleton, the drummer for the Temple of Doom," she said. "I mean, the *lead singer* for the Temple of Doom. Sorry, Carla!"

She turned to look at Carla, and for the first time noticed what her guest was wearing—a white leather T-shirt, a turquoise leather mini-skirt with metal studs, and thigh-high boots entirely covered with yellow feathers. "Wow!" Nancy said involuntarily. "What incredible boots! Where did you get them?"

For an awful moment Carla just stared, open-mouthed, at Nancy. Then she broke into easy laughter. "To tell you the truth, I wasn't ready for that question," she said. "Uh—Big Bird made them for me. No, actually, I made them myself. I bought the feathers at a warehouse and glued them on one at a time."

"But that must have taken forever!" Nancy exclaimed.

"Just about, but it was a perfect thing to do on the road. Gave me something to occupy myself on the bus. Some people do needlepoint, I glue feathers on boots. There's not much difference, really."

"I guess you're right," Nancy said. "But listen, Carla. You said you hadn't been expecting that question. What *were* you expecting, if you don't mind telling us?"

"Oh, something boring about what it's like being the only girl in the band. That's what people usually ask me."

"Well, we'll skip that, then," Nancy said. "What about—Oops! Wait, folks. One of the studio guys is giving me some kind of hand signal. I think—yes—you're about to see Temple of Doom's new video. Let's take a look."

"Okay, three minutes until you're back on, Nancy," said a cameraman. Everyone in the studio began talking at once.

The makeup woman rushed up to Nancy and began powdering her face. "Too bad we didn't get a chance to do this before," she said, "but I don't think anyone will notice. You're doing great."

Nancy was shaking all over. *"Great?"* she exclaimed. "All I did was goof up!" She turned to Carla. "I called you a drummer! I can't believe it!"

"Hey, it's okay," Carla said. "I'm having a good time. They'll see me sing on the video, anyway."

The makeup woman had finished, and now it was the hairdresser's turn. "Not much to do here," she said to Nancy. "We'll just mousse you up a tiny bit."

The cameraman was looking over the hairdresser's shoulder. "You're doing fine," he said reassuringly. "Very relaxed. Just make sure you don't turn away from the camera. Pretend it's a friend you're talking to."

"Carla, don't forget to mention the name of the new *album!*" came the frantic voice of Carla's agent.

"I will," said Carla calmly, *"if* it comes up. I don't have to talk about music *all* the time. If Nancy wants to talk about something else, that's fine with me."

"Okay, folks, back in places" came a technician's voice. "Nancy, keep up the good work."

The next twenty-two minutes passed in a blur. Nancy couldn't decide whether she was totally relaxed or more nervous than she'd ever been in her life. Whichever it was, she knew there was no point in trying to pretend she was totally comfortable in front of a camera—so she didn't try. And between commercials and switches to music videos, she managed to feel as though she were having a real conversation with Carla. They talked about everything, from what their high schools had been like to their favorite brands of ice cream.

When the show was over, everyone in the studio broke into applause—even Carla's agent.

All the lights came on, and Nancy looked out at the many faces that had been hidden by the dark. "Is that all?" she asked. "I don't get another chance?"

"You don't need one," the director said, walking up to her chair. "You came across completely naturally, and that's the most important thing."

"I hope Renee agrees with you," Nancy said, surprised and embarrassed when she started to yawn.

"It's perfectly natural," an assistant said. "It's the tension draining away."

Nancy smiled gratefully and peered around the studio. "Where is Renee? She was pretty upset with me just before the taping. I'd have thought she'd stick around to see how I did."

"She's probably tense because of the concert. In fact, she's probably *at* the stadium by now," a cameraman said.

"What concert?"

"The Crisp. They're at Featherstone Stadium tonight. I bet Renee left early to go with Vint."

"Vint Wylie?" Nancy asked. "She knows him?"

"*Knows* him! They've been going together for almost three years—ever since Jesse Slade disappeared."

"But I talked to—" Nancy stopped. She was supposed to be undercover and couldn't go around telling people she'd been talking to Vint Wylie!

The cameraman didn't notice Nancy's hesitation. "Renee doesn't mention it much around here," he said. "There's the thing about Jesse Slade."

"What thing about Jesse?"

"Well, you know that she was Jesse's girl before she started going out with Vint, right?"

"She *was?*" Nancy asked incredulously.

"Oh, yeah. They were quite an item. It didn't look too good when she started seeing Vint so soon after Jesse disappeared."

Suddenly he stopped. "Hey, what am I doing? I shouldn't be saying all this!"

"It's all right," Nancy assured him. "I won't tell anyone that you told me."

He seemed to perk up. "Okay," he said. "Anyway, I'm not telling you anything you wouldn't have found out sooner or later. Well, I've got to take off. Nice talking to you!"

Nice talking to *you,* Nancy thought. You've certainly added an interesting new angle to this case. And you've given me some pretty prime suspects, too.

No wonder Vint Wylie had lied about not knowing who Jesse Slade's girlfriend was. What if he and Renee had actually started seeing each other *before* Jesse died? Had they murdered Jesse?

Wait a minute, Nancy said to herself. Where's the motive? Could Renee and Vint be tied in to Tommy Road? Or did they have another reason to want Jesse dead?

Lost in thought, she walked slowly through the halls back to Renee's cubicle. She reached down

to pull her purse out from under Renee's desk—
and that's when she saw the note.

Please send Nancy Drew to my office
immediately.

Winslow Thomas

Instantly Nancy's heart began to pound. Had
Winslow seen her interview with Carla? Was he
angry?

When Nancy reached his office and saw his
grave face, she did not have her fears allayed.

"Sit down, Nancy," he said crisply. "I want to
talk to you. Hang on a second. I want Dan in
here, too."

Oh, no, Nancy thought.

Winslow picked up the phone. "Call Kennedy and get him in here," he ordered his
secretary. Then he hung up and turned to Nancy.

"You did a jolly good job interviewing Carla,"
Winslow said unexpectedly. Then he added,
"Considering your lack of preparation. You *were*
poised, but I think you'll agree that the whole
interview wasn't very, well, professional. I mean,
you certainly hadn't done your homework, had
you?"

What was Nancy supposed to say? She'd had
no time to do any "homework"—but she didn't
want to tell tales on Renee. Before she could
decide on an answer, Winslow spoke again.

"I also heard you were late this morning." He picked up a marble paperweight and began turning it in his hands, staring at it intently, unwilling to meet her eyes.

Finally he looked up. "What kind of progress are you making on your case?"

"Well, I—I have some leads, but—" Nancy knew she sounded as though she was floundering.

"But nothing definite," Winslow interrupted. "I thought that was what you'd say. Look, under the circumstances I can't justify having you here as a guest veejay any longer. I hate to say it, but I'm going to have to ask you to give up this case."

Chapter

Eight

BUT, MR. THOMAS, I've only been working for two days!" Nancy protested. "It always takes me a few days to start unraveling a case!"

"Be that as it may," Mr. Thomas said, "it's—well, disruptive having you here. Some members of my staff have started asking questions already. It hasn't escaped their attention that you came on as a guest veejay without coming through any of the normal channels. I can't fend off their questions much longer."

"But I—I don't understand why it would be bad if people knew who I was," Nancy said. "I'd think it would be good for TVR to get the credit for solving this mystery!"

"Not if the solution's unpleasant," Mr. Thomas countered swiftly. "And I'm afraid it will be."

"You wanted to see me, Mr. Thomas?" Dan Kennedy was poking his head into the room.

"Yes. Sit down. I've just been telling Nancy that I'd like her to stop investigating this matter with any help from us. I think it's doing the station a disservice. I wanted you to know, Dan," Winslow added wryly, "since you brought Nancy and her friends here in the first place."

Dan looked worried. Nancy couldn't blame him. Winslow wouldn't fire Dan because of her, would he?

She couldn't let that happen. She had to *prove* that Dan had been right in asking her to solve the mystery of Jesse's disappearance.

Nancy gathered up all her resolve. "Mr. Thomas," she said, "do you think you could give me another twenty-four hours here? If I don't have the case solved by then, I promise I'll forget it."

"I—I think that's a good idea," said Dan hesitantly. "I have complete confidence in Nancy, Mr. Thomas. She's been so busy since she got here that she really hasn't had any time to do much investigating."

Mr. Thomas met both of their eyes with his steely ones. Then quickly he stood, nodded his head, and said, "All right, Nancy. You've got your twenty-four hours. Use it well."

"Thank you," Nancy said with heartfelt relief. "Thank you very much. I do have an important lead I can follow up tomorrow morning." Last night she'd asked George to call Martin Rosenay, the dealer in Slade memorabilia, to set up an appointment with him for the next morning.

"I guess you'll be late tomorrow?" Mr. Thomas asked with a sly smile.

"I guess I will be," said Nancy, unconsciously holding her breath.

"Go ahead," said Mr. Thomas. "You can leave a note on Renee's desk and tell her I said it would be all right."

"I will. And thanks again, Mr. Thomas."

George and Bess were watching the evening news when Nancy walked into the bungalow and threw herself onto the couch. "I'm never moving again," she groaned.

"Can I get you a soda? Did you have another bad day?" George asked sympathetically.

Nancy sighed. "Yes, please, to the first question. Yes and no, to the second. It was interesting, at least." Quickly she filled George and Bess in on what had happened.

"At least you got to veejay. Do you have a tape?" Bess asked.

"Yes, they gave me one," Nancy said. "But I don't much feel like looking at it right now."

"I can't believe you didn't tell Mr. Thomas it was Renee's fault you weren't prepared!" Bess said. "Why are *you* taking all the blame for this?"

"Believe me, I *wanted* to tell him," Nancy said.

"But it just wouldn't be a good idea—especially now that she's a suspect. I don't want *her* to suspect that I suspect her, if you see what I mean. The nicer and more uncomplaining I am, the more relaxed she'll be around me."

"Well, you're just too much of a saint," Bess said. "But I suppose you're right."

"Did you two find out anything?" Nancy asked.

"Not that much," George said, "except that spending all day reading microfilm in a newspaper archive makes your eyes go crazy. I think I know every detail of the police investigation into Jesse's disappearance—"

"And I know every review of every song he ever released—" Bess put in.

"But nothing that looked like a clue," George finished.

Just then the phone rang. Nancy picked it up. "Hi, Nancy!" It was Dan Kennedy. "I just wanted to cheer you up."

"Well, I'm not feeling too great," Nancy admitted.

"Anything I can do to make you feel better? Are you free tomorrow morning after your appointment? Somebody canceled on me, and I've got a couple of hours open all of a sudden. I'd love an update on the case."

"Oh, Dan, I'm sorry. I'm going to be busy *all* morning," Nancy said regretfully. Then, from the corner of her eye, she saw Bess jumping up and down and pointing excitedly at herself and George. "But Bess and George are free," Nancy said. "Can they stand in for me?"

"Sure!" Dan said. "I'll take them to Fumetti's for breakfast. It's the latest hot spot. You know— mineral water and famous people."

"Sounds perfect," Nancy said with a laugh. "Should they meet you at TVR?"

"Sure. We'll go in my Lamborghini. It's my one luxury. I got it last year when my career took off. If it's worth doing, it's worth doing right— right?"

"Right. Thanks, Dan."

Nancy hung up and turned to her friends, smiling for the first time in hours. "We aim to please," she said.

The next morning Nancy dropped Bess and George off at the studio and stopped for a minute to admire Dan's car before heading to her appointment. She had just taken the exit for Chelmsford when her car phone suddenly began to ring. Astonished, she picked it up.

"Nancy? This is Lily, the receptionist at TVR. I'm sorry to bother you, but someone's just dropped off a package for you. There's a note on it that says it's urgent that you receive it immediately."

"A package? Who left it?"

"I don't know. I was away from my desk for a few minutes, and when I came back it was sitting here."

"Well, I'm on my way to an appointment that I really have to keep," Nancy said. "Could you possibly open it and tell me what it is?"

"Uh, gee, Nancy, I don't think I should," Lily answered uncertainly. "There's a sticker on it that says 'Private and Confidential.'"

"I see. Well, I guess I'd better come back, then," Nancy said. "Thanks, Lily."

Shaking her head in frustration, she turned and headed toward the freeway entrance that would take her back to the center of town.

She arrived at TVR, half an hour later, to find Lily looking terribly embarrassed.

"Nancy, you're not going to believe this," she said, "but I can't find the package. I was just on my way down to see if someone had taken it to Renee for you."

"I'll do that," Nancy said.

But there was no sign of the package in Renee's cubicle. And there was no sign of her package in the mailroom. Nancy checked on the off chance that it had been taken there by mistake. There was no sign of the package anywhere.

"I—I just don't know what happened," Lily said, faltering. "I went to the copy machine for a second to make some copies for Mr. Thomas, and when I came back, the package was gone! Do you think it was something important?"

"I hope not," Nancy said. She felt like screaming. A whole hour wasted, when she had so little time left! "Well, don't worry, Lily. It's not your fault." And she headed back out to her car.

Well, I've got to make the trip all over again, she thought to herself as she sat down in the driver's seat and switched on a classic-rock station. Then she headed out into the traffic.

She was just pulling into Martin Rosenay's long, gravel driveway when the radio suddenly stopped working—and the sound began.

A horrible, screeching, unbearably loud blast. A blast in full Sensurround blaring out through the car speakers, filling the car. And it grew even louder—and then unbelievably louder still.

Nancy had never felt a pain like the one assaulting her eardrums then. Black and red spots were dancing in front of her eyes, and her arms were shaking uncontrollably on the steering wheel. She fought desperately to keep the car under control, but the ear-shattering screech was finally too much for her. She doubled over in helpless agony—the steering wheel forgotten, her foot pressing down on the gas pedal.

The car swerved off the driveway, tossing up plumes of gravel before it crashed into the front of Martin Rosenay's house!

Chapter Nine

WITH A BONE-JARRING CRASH, the car came to a stop. But with the impact, the terrible sound stopped abruptly. White-faced and trembling, Nancy crawled out of the car and collapsed on her knees on the ground.

"Are you crazy? What do you think you're doing? You idiot—you should be locked up!"

Shakily Nancy stared up at the person who was yelling so furiously from the doorway. She saw a plump little man whose face was red with rage and whose whole body was quivering as he glared down at her.

"Mr.—Mr. Rosenay?" she whispered.

"That's right. And who are you?"

"I'm Nancy Drew." Nancy took a deep breath and pushed herself to her feet. But her legs were too weak to support her. She sagged against the hood of her car.

"I-I'm sorry," she said with tremendous effort. "There was something wrong with the—the speakers. It hurt so much that I—"

Now Martin Rosenay's manner changed completely. He jounced down the front steps and rushed up to her.

"That sound was coming from inside your car?" he asked in horror. "I was way in the back of the house, and even there it shattered my eardrums!"

"I think it did shatter mine," Nancy said. Her whole head was throbbing, and Rosenay's voice seemed to be coming from far off, under water.

"Well, it's no wonder you lost control of your car," he said contritely. "I apologize for yelling at you."

"My car! How badly is it damaged? And what about your *house?*"

Her pain pushed aside, Nancy rushed to the front of the car. She couldn't see the front bumper at all. It was buried in the bushes that lined the front of Rosenay's one-story ranch house.

"I'd better check this," Nancy said with a sinking feeling in her stomach. She climbed into the car and held her breath while turning the key. Would it start? The engine turned over once and died. Once again and this time it caught. Nancy backed it up a few feet. Then she got out to assess the damage.

"Only a couple of scratches! Thank heaven for rubber bumpers!" Nancy said.

Then she remembered: the house. What had the collision done to *it?*

Hastily, she stepped forward and pulled back the bushes in front of the house.

Nancy could hardly believe her eyes. There were a few scratches in the siding, but that was all.

"Well, it looks like minimal damage," she said after a second. "I must not have been going that fast—even though I felt like I was flying." I've got to find out how that radio was rigged, she thought to herself. Whoever did it really wanted me out of the way!

"Let's forget about it for the time being, then," Rosenay said. "A little paint will cover it all. Come on in!"

He led her up the front steps and through the door. "Welcome to Rosenay's Rock Memorabilia," he said.

Nancy could hardly believe her eyes. Every available surface—tables, chairs, sofas, and the floor—was covered with mementoes and souvenirs. There were heaps of old 45s and autographed pictures. There were buttons and T-shirts and hats and stickers and posters and fluorescent paintings on velvet and even models of Elvis Presley's tomb.

"Where do you *sit?*" Nancy asked.

Rosenay laughed. "I try not to," he answered. "You're interested in Jesse Slade stuff, I understand."

"That's right. I'm investigating his disappearance, and I just wondered whether there might possibly be any clues here."

"I don't know if there are or not, but come into the kitchen. All my Jesse things are on the kitchen table."

The kitchen was just as cluttered as the living room. "I guess you try not to eat, either?" Nancy said.

"Take-out. All I eat is take-out. Here's the Slade stuff," said Rosenay, gesturing toward the kitchen table. "Have a seat—wait, let me move this stuff." He shifted a pile of magazines from the chair to the floor.

There was a surprising amount of memorabilia, considering that Jesse Slade had been famous for such a short time before he'd disappeared. "I wouldn't have expected so much," Nancy said thoughtfully as she sat down and began leafing through a pile of photos and articles.

Rosenay looked a little uncomfortable. "I've got a great supplier," he answered. "He's in touch with all the Jesse Slade fan clubs—there were about sixty, you know."

"How much of it do you sell?" asked Nancy.

"To be frank, not a whole lot—not yet," answered Rosenay. "I get a few letters a week or so, but mostly I think of this particular collection as an investment."

"Did you know Jesse at all?" Nancy asked.

"Pretty well. No, that's an exaggeration, I guess. Let's say I know people who knew him pretty well. Your friend said you were an investigator. Do you have any ideas about what happened to Jesse?"

"I've got a few. I'm not ruling anything out," Nancy said carefully. "*You* don't have any ideas about what happened to him, do you?"

"Oh, I have ideas. Everyone has ideas," said Rosenay. His chubby face suddenly became veiled. "I don't want to point the finger at anyone, but if I were you I'd ask Renee Stanley and Vint Wylie to explain a few things. Like why they were seeing each other on the sly before Jesse disappeared, and why neither of them seemed very upset once he was gone. It just doesn't seem quite right to me, that's all."

"Do you really think they plotted together to make him disappear?" Nancy asked.

"Off the record? Yes, I think that's exactly what happened," answered Rosenay.

"But is that a real motive?" Nancy put down the stack of photos she was holding. She'd been worrying about the motive ever since she'd first begun to suspect Renee. "I mean, if they wanted to go out together, all Renee had to do was break up with Jesse. It might have been a little awkward —but not nearly as awkward as risking a murder charge!"

"Look, *I'm* not the investigator," Rosenay replied. "All I know is, I watched a local-TV news interview with Renee just after Jesse had disappeared. She didn't mention Vint—even though everybody in the business knew about him. And she kept referring to Jesse in the past tense. Now, why would she do that unless she knew he was dead?"

"Good point," Nancy said. She bent her head to a stack of photos. "I'd better start looking through this stuff. I'm sure you don't have all day."

"Make yourself comfortable," Rosenay said. "I'll be out back putting in my tomato plants."

For the next half hour Nancy sifted through the piles in front of her. There were lots of letters from Jesse to his fans—probably collected from the fan clubs, she thought—and dozens of pictures and fan magazines featuring him. But no clues leapt out at her.

At last she stood up and walked out back. "Mr. Rosenay?" she said. "I think I'm done."

He put down his trowel and stood up, brushing the dirt off his hands. "Find anything?"

"Not really," Nancy said. "But if it's all right, I'd love to borrow a picture of Jesse to take with me. I'll bring it back, of course."

"No need for that," said Rosenay. "I'll donate it to the cause. I hope you find out what happened to him."

"That's very nice of you," said Nancy. "Is it okay to take this one?"

It was a photo of Jesse Slade standing in front of his car. He was laughing at something off-camera, and he looked totally relaxed.

"He looks so happy here," Nancy said. "I guess that's why this is my favorite of all the ones you have."

"He does, doesn't he?" For a second the two of them stared at the picture in silence. "You're welcome to it," Rosenay said. "And give me a call if there's anything more I can help you with."

"I sure will. Thanks, Mr. Rosenay," said Nancy sincerely.

He walked with her to the front of the house and watched as she got into her car. "Careful, now," he said anxiously.

"Don't worry," Nancy replied. "Your house is safe from me!"

Feeling more cheerful than she had when she'd set out that morning, she headed back to TVR. This time, she kept the radio turned off.

Bess and George were waiting for her in Dan's office when she got back. "We were hoping you'd get here soon. Oh, Nancy! We had the greatest time!" Bess exclaimed when she saw her. "The restaurant was so good—and there were all *kinds* of stars having 'power breakfasts'—and Dan's the coolest guy in the world! Thanks so much for taking this case! Did you find out anything at that guy's house?"

"Well, nothing too specific," Nancy answered, "but he did give me a few ideas—and this picture." She took the picture out of its envelope and held it out to her friends.

"Nice," George commented. "Hey, that's a different color, but it's just like Dan's car."

Nancy went to George's side and stared at the picture again. Then she snatched it out of her friend's hands.

"Rosenay knows where Jesse is!" she gasped. "This picture proves it!"

Chapter

Ten

Y OU'RE RIGHT, GEORGE—it *is* just like Dan's car!" Nancy said angrily. "Dan bought his a year ago! Jesse's car is a Lamborghini, too, so this has to be *last year's model!"*

"Last year's model? But that means . . ." Bess began.

"Right, Bess," said Nancy. "It means Jesse was around last year. And *that* means he's probably still around now! Jesse could even be the 'friend' Martin Rosenay talked about—that would make sense. And Rosenay may be keeping his whereabouts a secret so that he can corner the market in Jesse Slade memorabilia. To think that I trusted him! And Jesse—why is he hiding out?"

"Are you *sure* about all this?" asked Bess.

"As sure as I can be without Jesse standing here. I can try to trace the license plate—too bad Jesse's standing in front of the second half of it. I'm sure that car is no more than a year old."

"Well, what are you going to do?" asked George calmly.

"I'm going right back there and tell Rosenay— No, wait. I can't do that." Nancy stopped pacing. "I've got to stay here. If I have only until tonight before I have to leave TVR, I'd better not waste any time. I'll go down and see if Renee's in and if she can use me for anything."

"What about us?" asked Bess.

"Let's see . . . I can't think of anything right now, guys. I guess you'd better take the afternoon off and go shopping."

But Bess was frowning. "Ordinarily you know I'd take you up on that like a shot, Nan. But don't you think you could use us for something around here? If it's your last day and all—"

Nancy felt very touched. Even if she never managed to solve this case, it was great to have such good friends. "That's nice of you, Bess," she said. "I really can't come up with anything at the moment, but why don't you two come down to Renee's office with me? I could use some moral support when I talk to her."

"Fine," George said. "And if she has any filing or something to do, *we'll* do it."

When the three friends got to Renee's office,

she wasn't there. "She's in the conference room down the hall," a man said as he walked by and saw them. "I just saw her in there."

Renee didn't notice them walk in. She was too busy watching a tape of some concert—and when Nancy looked more closely, she saw Vint Wylie on the screen. It must be the concert from the night before.

"Hi, Renee," Nancy said, plunking herself down next to the veejay. "What are you watching?"

"Oh! You startled me!" Renee whirled around with an irritable scowl.

"It's just a tape of the Crisp concert from last night," she told Nancy. "I was watching it to see—uh, to see whether we could use any of it."

"And to see Vint, right?" Nancy asked. Behind them, Bess and George silently sat down. "You two *are* going out, aren't you?"

"That's none of your business," Renee snapped.

"Well, I guess I should level with you. I'm a private investigator," Nancy said, and Renee's jaw dropped. "I didn't really come to TVR as a guest veejay. I'm looking into Jesse's disappearance." I don't have to mince words, she told herself. There's no reason why I need to stay on Renee's good side anymore. "I was surprised to find out that you and Vint are going out."

"Do you know Vint?" Renee asked cautiously.

"I talked to him yesterday," Nancy said.

"You *talked* to Vint?" Renee whispered.

"Uh-huh. But he didn't mention that the two of you had been together for three years. Didn't he mention that I'd come by?" Nancy continued.

Renee shook her head.

"I wonder why not," Nancy said thoughtfully.

"He—he probably didn't want to worry me."

"*Worry* you? About what?" Nancy asked.

"Well, he knows I get pretty upset whenever—whenever anybody asks about Jesse. I— He wouldn't have wanted me to know that someone was stirring the whole thing up again." Renee drew in a shaky breath.

"And is there any reason you didn't mention that you and Vint had been seeing each other?" Nancy continued implacably. "It's not a secret, is it?"

"N-no," Renee stammered. "But we never—" She cleared her throat. "I— Well, it's just a little bit awkward. That's really the only reason I try to downplay it. You know, a veejay and a musician going out . . . people might get the idea there were possibilities for—well, conflict of interest."

"I can see how they might," Nancy said. "I haven't had time to check Jesse's will yet, Renee. Is there anything in it I should know about?"

Renee was scowling now. "What is this—a firing squad? Oh, all right," she muttered after a second. "Yes. He left me some money."

There was a little pause. "Oh, I know what you're thinking, Nancy!" Renee burst out. "But Vint and I don't know what happened to Jesse. We really don't! You have to believe me!"

"Why?" was all Nancy said.

"Because—because—why would we do something like that?" Renee was twisting her hands together so hard that her knuckles were white. "It's true that we didn't tell Jesse we'd started going out—but that doesn't mean we'd kill him! And he wasn't going to leave me *that* much!"

"I didn't mention killing him!" Nancy said sharply. "Do you think he *was* killed?"

"Why, of course I do. I mean, what else could have happened? How could he still be alive?" Renee's eyes were enormous in her white face. She leaned forward and grabbed Nancy's wrist painfully hard. *"He isn't alive, is he?"* she almost shrieked.

"I'm not sure, Renee." Gently Nancy pulled Renee's clawing hand off her wrist. "But I never rule out anything."

"Oh, no," Renee said breathily. "It can't be!" She stood up on shaky legs. "I-I'm on in fifteen minutes," she said. "I don't want to be late." And she walked slowly from the room.

"If Jesse is alive, what's Renee worried about?" Nancy asked out loud. Unless—unless she thought she'd killed him herself—

Nancy gave herself a mental shake. "I'm wasting time sitting here speculating about all this," she said. "I bet Renee knows more than she's saying." She leaned forward to switch off the tape in the VCR, and then paused. "I can't resist watching Vint for a second," she said.

The Crisp was the kind of group that was really proud of being down-to-earth and unflashy. They never wore anything fancier than T-shirts and jeans, they never used any lighting effects fancier than a strobe, and they always sang songs about ordinary working-class people. Nancy didn't follow them much—she actually thought they were a little boring—but they'd been topping the charts for six months now. Vint certainly knew how to pick people to play with!

There he was in back, brandishing a two-necked white bass guitar and looking much more wide-awake than when Nancy had talked to him in person. He appeared to be unconscious of the camera—except that he had an uncanny knack for always facing it. Even when the concert ended and the band took a bow, Vint angled his body slightly toward the camera instead of the crowd. Very subtle scene stealing.

The audience screamed in disappointment when it finally became clear that the band wasn't going to do another encore. Once again Nancy leaned forward to turn off the tape—and once again she stopped. The tape had just cut to what was obviously a huge post-concert party at Vint's house.

"Hey!" said George. "Let's watch this for a second, too! Bess never got a chance to see what Vint's house was like."

As she watched, Nancy saw that all the trees on Vint's property had been covered with tiny hot-pink lights, and the swimming pool was ringed with potted tropical trees of all kinds. There was Renee on Vint's arm. He was wearing jeans, but she was in a skin-tight strapless leather mini dress.

The camera focused in on a waiter's tray next. It was full of tiny hollowed-out potatoes filled with caviar. As Nancy watched, a woman's hand with fluorescent green nails reached in and picked one up.

Then the scene shifted to Vint's front yard, where what looked like an entire precinct of private security guards was directing traffic and keeping out gate crashers. Behind a barricade was a crowd of people trying to get a glimpse of the party, and behind them was a mess of cars trying to get through.

Poor guys, Nancy thought. It must be really maddening to get stuck in the middle of party traffic.

But wait! What car was that?

The car Nancy noticed was nosing slowly up to

the edge of the crowd. It was impossible to see the driver, but the first half of the license-plate number looked awfully familiar. And the car itself was a white Lamborghini—last year's model.

"That must be Jesse!" Nancy gasped.

Chapter

Eleven

"THAT PARTY was last night!" said Nancy. "If Jesse was there, then that means he can't be that far away! We've got to find him!"

"Where are you going? What about Renee?" asked Bess as Nancy jumped to her feet.

"We'll worry about her later," said Nancy. "There's one person who I'm *sure* knows where Jesse is—and that's Martin Rosenay. Let's get out to his house right away!"

Nancy was almost out the door when she suddenly remembered something else. "Let's get all of Jesse's license-plate number from the tape," she said. "If Rosenay won't talk, we might still be able to track Jesse down. At least I hope so. We *can't* let him get away when we're this close to him!"

The three girls dashed out of the studio and into their car. Miraculously, the traffic wasn't too bad and they reached Chelmsford quickly to find a car in Martin Rosenay's driveway. With a screech of brakes Nancy stopped behind it and jumped out. "Come on," she said over her shoulder to Bess and George. "Let's get this over with."

The three girls stalked up the front path, and Nancy rapped loudly on the door. In a second Martin Rosenay appeared, wiping his mouth with a napkin. He was carrying a huge bowl of chocolate ice cream.

"Nancy!" he exclaimed. "And?" he asked, looking at Bess and George.

"These are my friends, George Fayne and Bess Marvin," Nancy said, making the introductions fast.

"Come in, come in! Wait, let me put this down somewhere. Let's see. Where?" Rosenay asked himself, looking for any place that wasn't piled high with memorabilia. "Don't want it to spill on anything—the fans would *not* go for that." He chuckled. "I can just see telling them the picture they wanted was—"

"It's the picture we're here about, Mr. Rosenay," Nancy interrupted. "The one of Jesse that you gave me."

He looked startled. "What about it? I said you could keep it, didn't I?"

"Yes, you did," Nancy replied. "But I'm surprised. Are you sure you wanted me to have such a recent picture of Jesse?"

"A what? What do you mean?" Suddenly Rosenay didn't look quite so cheerful.

"I mean that can't be an old picture. I mean that picture was taken only last year. I mean that Jesse Slade is still very much alive and living very near here."

Rosenay just stared at her.

"Let me refresh your memory," Nancy said.

She reached into her bag and pulled out the picture. "Whoever shot this must not have known anything about cars," she said, pointing to the Lamborghini in the picture. "This model is not three years old! You've been running a pretty good scam, Mr. Rosenay—but now it's time to stop."

"Let me see that picture," Mr. Rosenay said in a ghost of his usual voice. Slowly he reached out and took it from Nancy's hand. He stared at it for a second, then collapsed onto a pile of letters in a nearby chair.

"You could be right," he whispered. "Maybe he *is* still alive." Still staring at the picture, he absentmindedly took a spoonful of ice cream. "But who would have guessed?"

"You mean *you* didn't know?" Bess burst out.

Rosenay shook his head. "I didn't. I didn't think he was still alive. I thought some of my pictures might possibly be fakes—but I thought they'd been made with a Jesse Slade look-alike. Not the real Jesse!

"I know—I know what you're going to say," he said when he saw Nancy's expression. "I shouldn't have sold them if I thought they weren't genuine.

"But look at it from my point of view," he went on. "Jesse memorabilia may get really big one day. And when I suddenly started hearing from a supplier who could give me all kinds of stuff, including great pictures, I couldn't resist. Sometimes I did wonder if the pictures were fakes, but I didn't *know* for sure. Was I supposed to rock the boat?"

"Yes," George said bluntly.

Rosenay gave her a sad smile and a shrug. "Maybe," he said, "but you don't know what it's like trying to earn a living in this business. Also, I didn't want my supplier getting in trouble. I was thinking about protecting him—if you can believe it."

Nancy could almost believe it, but not quite. She'd liked Rosenay when she first met him, but now she wasn't sure how she felt. But one thing was certain—he was definitely out for himself.

"I'd like to believe you, Mr. Rosenay," she

said, "and I would like your help now. You can't protect your supplier any longer—not if he knows the truth about Jesse. It's our duty to inform the world if Jesse's still alive."

Nancy didn't mention the fact that she thought Jesse himself was probably the "supplier." That wasn't information she wanted him to have. "You can understand that, can't you?"

"Sure," he said after a minute. He stood up decisively. "Let me get this stupid ice cream out of my hands"—he took one more bite—"and I'll go and find the shipment that that picture came in. I haven't cataloged it yet."

"This is an incredible place," Bess whispered when Rosenay had left. "How can he give up his living room like this?"

"It's not just his living room; it's the whole house," Nancy whispered back. "The Jesse Slade things are in the kitchen. I hope he can *find* the shipment he's looking for."

From the sounds coming from the kitchen, Nancy decided Rosenay was having trouble. There were several thuds as though he'd dropped some boxes, an "ouch!" and then the unmistakable noise of a pile of papers slithering to the ground.

At last Rosenay reappeared, clutching a large manila envelope. "I think these are the ones," he said. "Let's hope so. I kind of tore the place up looking for them."

Eagerly Nancy took the envelope. It was

postmarked Los Gatos, California. "No address, I suppose," she said to Rosenay.

"No. Just a post office box—box forty-six. But Los Gatos is tiny—it shouldn't be hard to track someone down there."

"I hope you're right," Nancy said, taking a stack of photos out of the envelope and dividing them among the three of them. "Just look through these for a sec," she said.

"What are we looking for?" George wanted to know.

"I'm not sure. Background details, I guess. Anything that might tell us where the pictures were taken."

It was eerie seeing so many pictures of Jesse Slade and knowing that he must be alive after all. *I wonder who knows about him besides us?* Nancy thought. *Can it be possible that we're the only ones?* She shivered suddenly.

Bess must have been thinking along the same lines. She looked up from her stack of pictures and said, "I should think it would be lonely, having no one know you're *you.*"

"Maybe so," Nancy said. "Have you guys noticed anything? Because I haven't."

"I haven't, either," said Bess, and George shook her head.

"Then we'll just have to go out to Los Gatos and see what we can find," Nancy said. "And we'd better get going. The afternoon's going to be gone before we know it."

"And we haven't had lunch yet. . . ." Bess said plaintively.

"After that giant breakfast?" George asked, amazed that Bess was hungry already.

"We'll pick up something on the way," Nancy answered to keep peace. "Mr. Rosenay, thanks."

"No problem," he said a little sheepishly. "I hope you find him."

"What a gorgeous town Los Gatos is," Bess said gloomily half an hour later. "Really, Nancy, you do take us to the glamor spots!"

"Welcome to Los Gatos—Pop. 182," said the fly-specked sign just outside town. It was hard to believe such a dusty little place could be just an hour outside of Los Angeles. Los Gatos looked more like a ghost town in an old western movie than anything else—hot, dirty, and empty. There was even an old dog sleeping lazily in the middle of the road in front of the post office.

Carefully Nancy steered her car around him. "We might as well ask someone at the post office whether they can help us," she said, "since the gas station is closed."

A woman reading a magazine behind the counter looked up in mild surprise as the girls trooped in.

"Afternoon, ladies," she said. "May I help you with something?"

"Well, it's a little complicated," said Nancy.

"We're looking for the address of one of your boxholders. The box number is forty-six."

"Let's see." The woman put down her magazine, heaved herself to her feet, and ran her finger down a list of names on the wall. "Mr. Joplin, that is," she said. "Out on Horse Pasture Road. Take a right at the stop sign out front and drive for about a quarter of a mile. You'll see Horse Pasture on your left. It's a dirt road, and his house is the only one on it. You can't miss it."

"Thank you so much," said Nancy. "We really appreciate it."

"We're lucky this is such a small town," she said to George and Bess once they were safely back in the car. "In a bigger place I don't think she'd have given us the address like that."

"Well, we don't exactly look like dangerous criminal types," said George. "She probably knew she could trust us. Look, there's the turn. We're here at last!"

The modest gray house at the end of the road seemed to huddle forlornly in the shade of the steep hill behind it. Shades had been drawn across most of the windows, and the lawn had gone to seed.

Nancy's heart was pounding as she switched off the ignition and heard the refrain of a wailing guitar float out an open window. The three girls slid out of the car. Nancy couldn't place the melody. I know I've heard it recently, she said to herself. But when?

Then she remembered. It had been the night they'd been watching television at Bess's. It seemed so long ago now! The song was "Goodbye, Sweet Life," and it was turned up to top volume on the stereo.

The melody broke off in the middle, then started up again. It wasn't a record. *Someone inside was actually playing the song.*

Nancy pressed the front doorbell, and the music stopped in the middle of a measure. She heard footsteps move toward them.

The man who answered the door looked thin, and his jeans and grubby T-shirt were threadbare. He looked as if he hadn't shaved for a couple of days. But all three girls recognized him right away.

"You're—you're—" Nancy had trouble getting the words out.

"Yeah," said the man with the crooked grin. "I'm Jesse Slade."

Chapter

Twelve

"So SOMEONE FOUND ME at last," said Jesse Slade. "I knew it had to happen sometime."

The face that had smiled out from millions of record covers was now staring suspiciously at the three girls. "Can I do something for you, now that you're here?"

Nancy found her voice. "I'm a private investigator. Could we possibly talk to you for a few minutes?"

"Depends," said Jesse. "What are you planning to do with whatever I tell you?"

"I—I don't know yet," said Nancy. "I haven't thought about that, actually. I guess it depends on *what* you tell us."

Slade shrugged. "That's honest, anyway. Come on in."

He led them into what Nancy guessed would have been called the living room if it had had any real furniture. There were two tattered armchairs, a television, an electric piano, a stereo and compact-disk player, and an amplifier.

"It's a little primitive in here," Slade apologized. "I hope you don't mind. Let's see—two of you can have the chairs, one can have the piano bench, and I'll take the floor."

Nancy took the piano bench. From there she could see most of the other rooms in the house. All of them were furnished, or not furnished, like the living room. The walls were bare, the floors were bare. There were no homey touches—it all looked as though Jesse Slade had just moved in.

"How long have you lived here?" she asked.

"Going on three years," Jesse answered. "Ever since—ever since I disappeared." He looked around as if seeing the place with an outsider's eyes. "It still needs fixing up, I guess. I just can't seem to get around to it.

"Well!" he continued. "What brings the three of you to my doorstep?"

"My name's Nancy Drew," Nancy said, "and I'm a private investigator. These are my friends Bess Marvin and George Fayne." Jesse nodded at them. Bess just stared, open-mouthed and wide-eyed. George did return his nod.

"We were watching a TVR special—you know

what TVR is, right?" He nodded again. "A TVR special about your last concert, and I noticed some movement, what looked like a body falling off a cliff just beside and behind the stage. We began wondering if maybe you had fallen off that cliff."

"So someone finally noticed that," Jesse said grimly. "It sure took long enough. I decided that maybe the cameras hadn't caught the actions."

"It was on the tape, but a good tape wasn't found until very recently," Nancy told him. "And it was just by accident that I saw the fall. It was very dark, and I only saw it because of the movement. Anyway, Bess called TVR, and they agreed to let me use the station as a base of operations while we looked for you. And—here we are.

"We thought you could have been hurt," she went on. "That's why we decided to investigate in the first place. If someone had hurt you—or even killed you—and there was some way to catch that person . . ."

"But I'm that person," Jesse said softly.

The three girls stared at him, not understanding.

"*I was* involved in that accident on the cliff." he said. "But I wasn't the one who fell."

Nancy's mouth was dry.

"*I* knocked *him* off. My manager, Tommy Road. We were yelling at each other. I took a step toward him—I guess I must have looked pretty

105

scary—and he stepped backward. The cliff crumbled under him, and he went down." Jesse didn't speak for a long minute. "Did he die, do you know?"

His eyes were fixed on Nancy's with painful intensity. "I don't know," Nancy said. "No one knows. He never turned up after that night—he disappeared just like you."

Slowly Jesse let out his breath. "So I'll never know if I'm responsible for his death or not."

"Jesse," Nancy said gently, "maybe you'd better start at the beginning."

"Okay," he said after drawing in a ragged breath. "You probably know that my career was going pretty well before that concert."

That broke the tension in the room, somehow. All four of them laughed. *Pretty* well," George said.

"Yeah. Well, I guess that is an understatement. And a whole lot of the credit has to go to Tommy Road. He took a chance on me when no one else would. He practically never slept, trying to get someone in the industry to listen to me—and when Clio Records finally signed me, he got me just about the best deal in recording history."

He stood up and stared out the window at the drab view outside. "But after a while I began to suspect that Tommy wasn't being exactly straight with me. It's partly my fault, I know. I mean, I *let* him take control of my money, just the way he took control of my career. I didn't want to be bothered with financial details. I hate numbers and making boring phone calls to accountants and things like that. And he was great at it.

"But every now and then I'd wonder where the money was all going. He said he was investing it for me." Jesse gave a short laugh. "Funny way of investing it—funneling it into his own account."

"I found out about that, too," Bess put in timidly. "I checked your general ledger at Lawrence Associates."

"Yeah, that's what I finally did, too. And I figured it all out the day before that last concert. I was furious, as you can imagine. My own manager—the guy who'd been like my best friend for *years*—embezzling from me practically since day one!

"I didn't have a chance to talk to him about it until the night of the concert," Jesse went on. "That gave me a lot of time to decide what to say. When I took my break, I found Tommy and said that I was never going to perform again unless he returned every dollar. I figured that would scare him. You know—that he wouldn't want to lose his biggest client.

"But it turned out he'd been waiting for this," Jesse said savagely. "Tommy told *me* he didn't want to be my manager any longer! He said he was going to leave the country—*with* all my money—and that I'd never see a cent of what he'd taken. On top of that, he started insulting me for not having noticed what was going on before then. . . ."

Jesse's voice faltered. "So I took a step toward him. I don't know if I meant to punch him or what. He—he went down without a sound, just like something in a nightmare. I was terrified to look down over the edge. I was afraid of what I might see. It must have only been a couple of seconds, but it seemed like hours before I looked down." He closed his eyes as if the memory was too painful for him to stand. "Then I looked. There was his body lying down there, all crumpled up on the rocks."

Bess winced.

"I looked around the stage," Jesse continued. *"No one had noticed a thing!* My backup band was still playing, and all the technicians were running around setting up for the finale. If I'd wanted to, I could just have gone back and rejoined the band, and maybe no one would ever have found out what had happened. But I couldn't do it. Even though he'd been cheating me, I couldn't leave him down there."

"So you climbed down after him?" Nancy said.

"Right. Boy, I had plenty of time to think about how he must have felt going down! It was pitch dark, and the wind was whipping around, and pieces of the cliff kept crumbling under my feet. . . .

"But when I got down to the bottom—down to where the rocks were—the body was gone. A wave must have come in and carried it out."

Jesse sighed. "So there I was. And right then I decided to take off for Mexico. No way could I go back up there without people realizing something had happened—and I couldn't stand the thought of facing a murder charge. I had about two hundred dollars in my pocket. I walked down the beach for about an hour, then climbed up another part of the cliff, found a road, and started hitchhiking. I crossed the border into Mexico the next day."

"No one recognized you?" George asked.

"Nope. You know, people don't usually recognize famous people unless they're expecting to see them. They usually just think, 'Gee, that sure looks like so-and-so.' Once in a while someone would say how much I looked like Jesse Slade"—he smiled—"and I'd just tell them I'd heard that before."

"But how have you been living since then?" Nancy asked.

"In Mexico things were pretty hand-to-mouth for a few months, until I got a job as a waiter. I scraped up enough money to buy a guitar, and when I could afford to come back here I started giving lessons. But I don't do that too much. Mostly I do odd jobs. I'm a caretaker for the big house back up the road. The owner's great. He lets me use the pickup parked outside."

Nancy happened to glance over at Bess, who looked as if she were wilting in her chair. Nancy was sure she was crushed that her idol had sunk so low. But to Nancy, it didn't sound as if Jesse was unhappy about the direction his life had taken.

"You don't seem to mind your obscurity and poverty too much," she commented.

Jesse thought about it for a second. "Nope. I guess I don't," he said thoughtfully. "It's a relief not having everyone look up to me—and not feeling as if I'm responsible for making a million fans happy. Having all those girls in love with me got kind of—kind of exhausting." Bess looked up, a little startled.

"Well, I've managed to fool everyone till now," Jesse said. "How did you finally find me?"

Nancy explained about Martin Rosenay, and Jesse grimaced. "Of course. Of *course,*" he said. "I should have known that car would get me in trouble. It belongs to the guy whose house I take care of."

"Who took the pictures, by the way?" George asked.

"I did. I gave some guitar lessons in exchange for a secondhand Nikon. I cleaned myself up, set the timer, and started posing. Selling the pictures was an easy way to get cash."

"I wonder what did happen to Tommy Road," Nancy said thoughtfully. "Is it possible that he's still alive? It seems hard to believe that his body was never found. The police combed that whole site so carefully. What if he survived the fall? What if he slid down the cliff instead of falling?"

"I guess he could have gone underground like me," Jesse said. "And he was such a crook that he's probably managed to do a lot better for himself than I have," he added bitterly.

Silence fell. Suddenly the little house seemed as remote and forgotten as Jesse Slade himself.

"What are you going to do now that you've found me?" he suddenly asked.

Nancy stared at him. "I don't know. I just don't know," she said. "I don't blame you for what happened, and you're not a murderer. What do you *want* me to do? I'm sure that if you came forward with your story, people would believe you. The general ledger will bear you out—"

"No. I don't want to come forward," Jesse said in a strained voice. "I don't want to live in that fishbowl again. I'm all right where I am, and I'm not bothering anyone. Please, Nancy," he begged, "can't you leave this alone? Can't you forget you ever saw me, and not tell anyone where I am?"

Nancy looked from him to Bess and George. Almost imperceptibly they nodded.

"All right, Jesse," Nancy said. "We'll go back to L.A. And we won't tell anyone about you, except the people at TVR. I think I can promise that they'll keep it confidential, and I really owe it to them."

"Thank you," Jesse said. "Thank you more than I can say."

"You're welcome," Nancy said, getting to her feet. "I guess we'll be on our—"

Just then they heard a car door slamming, quickly followed by footsteps coming up the walk. Then there was a frantic knock at the front door.

Everyone froze. "You expecting anyone else?" Jesse muttered.

The knock sounded again, even louder this time. Jesse strode forward and opened the door.

A blinding burst of light exploded in his face!

Chapter

Thirteen

JESSE STAGGERED BACKWARD, his hands covering his face. Another strobe light went off, and another and another, as if someone had hurled a bunch of silent firecrackers into the house.

Now the three girls could see the reporter framed in the doorway, a cameraman at his back. He jammed a microphone into Jesse's face. "You're Jesse Slade, aren't you?" he asked. "I'm from Channel Six. What a story this will make! Hey, who are the girls?"

"Get out of here!" Jesse shouted, hurling himself against the door. Quickly he slipped the bolt shut. Then he leaned against the door, breathing hard.

"You didn't tell anyone you were coming here, did you?" he asked Nancy.

"No, except for—except for Martin Rosenay," Nancy said. All of a sudden she knew exactly what had happened.

So did Jesse. "Rosenay! Of course! He must have finally figured out that I was the supplier. He'd do anything to sell that junk of his. He must have called all the press in town, that little—" He stopped. "Well, there's certainly no reason for you to keep quiet *now.*"

"I guess not," Nancy agreed quietly. "I'm so sorry, Jesse. I hope you know I didn't expect things to turn out this way."

"Oh, I know," said Jesse. More cheerfully, he added, "It could never have lasted, anyway. I always told myself that. And maybe I can fend them off for a while, at least long enough for me to track down a lawyer."

"Good idea," said Nancy. "And speaking of tracking down people—I'd better call Mr. Thomas at TVR and let him know what's happened."

"Why?" Jesse inquired. "He's sure to find out soon enough, the way things are going!"

"Yes, but it wouldn't be fair to let this kind of news catch him unprepared," said Nancy. "He'll have every reason to be angry at me if the regular networks scoop him. I'm not saying he'll send reporters out here," she added hastily when she saw Jesse's face, "but he should know."

But Mr. Thomas's personal line was busy. It was busy a couple of minutes later when Nancy tried again, and a couple of minutes after that. At last she gave up.

"We'll just drive back and tell him in person," she said. "Is there a back door?"

"In the kitchen." Jesse led the way, but just before Nancy opened the door he put out a hand to stop her. "Do you three think you can come back later?" he asked almost shyly. "It would be nice to have some supporting troops around. I have a feeling this is all going to get pretty heavy."

"Sure," Nancy said immediately. "It's really the least we can do. Okay, Bess and George, when I open the door, run for the car. And don't answer any questions."

They were almost to the car when the reporter at the front door saw them. "Girls! Girls!" he shouted, racing toward them. "What were you doing in there? Where's he been all this time?"

"No comment," Nancy said firmly as they clambered into their seats. Frantically the reporter beckoned to the cameraman to come and join him in front of the car. "You'd better get out of the way when I start this thing," Nancy muttered under her breath.

To her relief, the reporter and cameraman scuttled out of the way once the engine turned over.

"Okay, we're off," Nancy said.

"You solved the case, Nan," Bess said. But she didn't sound too enthusiastic about it.

"Yes," Nancy agreed wearily. "And I'm not sure that's a good thing at all."

"And he's been living there all this time?" Winslow Thomas asked in amazement.

"That's right," said Nancy. "Giving guitar lessons and being a caretaker."

"Well, blow me down," said Mr. Thomas, and he really did sound as though someone *had* blown him down. He sat at his desk a moment, considering—and then stood up and shook Nancy's hand vigorously.

"Very impressive work, Nancy," he said. "As you know, I had my doubts, but you're obviously very good at what you do. Congratulations."

"Thank you," Nancy began. "I'm happy to have cleared up *one* aspect of this case, anyway. But Mr. Thomas, do you think you could possibly downplay this story for a few days? I know it's big news for a station like yours, but Jesse seems—well, he seems a little out of it. I think it would be unkind to make him talk now."

"I think you're right," said Mr. Thomas. "Let's be as kind as possible to the poor blighter." Where does he get these odd expressions? Nancy wondered irrelevantly. "I tell you what," Mr. Thomas went on. "I've got an appointment now, but before I go I'll have my secretary call a meeting of all the TVR executives so that we can decide how to handle this story. First of all, we'll schedule a press conference. When Jesse's feeling more on top of things—"

"Jesse who?"

It was Renee. She and Vint Wylie were standing in the office doorway—and both of them looked as though they'd seen a ghost.

"What are you doing here, Renee?" Mr. Thomas snapped. "I thought you weren't on today."

"I'm not," Renee said in a strangled voice. "Vint and I just stopped in to pick up something I'd forgotten. Mr. Thomas, wh-who are you talking about?"

"Well, I have to confess I wasn't going to tell the staff yet," said Mr. Thomas, "but it seems Jesse Slade has come back to life."

"Oh, no!" Renee put her hand to her throat. "I—I can't breathe!" she cried. "This is terrible!"

And she burst into tears. "I can't handle this!" she cried, and raced out of the office.

"Renee! Wait!" Vint called, rushing after her.

Mr. Thomas shook his head. "These temperamental stars!" he said with a chuckle. "Well, I'm off." He gave them a cheery wave as he disappeared down the hall.

"I wonder if Dan's around," Bess said hopefully. "He should hear about this, don't you think?"

"I definitely think so," Nancy said. "Let's go to his office and see."

Dan *was* in, and he was as amazed by their story as Mr. Thomas had been.

"The poor, poor guy," he said, shaking his head. "When you think of what he's been through—he's got to feel totally shell shocked. Look, Nancy, do me a favor. If he wants somewhere to stay until all the publicity dies down, will you give him my address?" He was scribbling it down as he spoke. "I won't call him and bother him, but tell him he can call me or come by any time he wants."

"That's great, Dan," Nancy said warmly. "I wouldn't be surprised if he takes you up on it. We're heading back there now, and I'll tell him first thing."

"What time is it?" George asked as they passed the sign for Los Gatos. "I feel as if we've been doing nothing but drive for about ten hours."

"It's six," Nancy replied. "We'll just check in with Jesse, and then we can go back to the hotel and call it a day."

"And get some supper," Bess interjected.

"And get some supper," said Nancy. "Oh, no. What's going *on?*"

She'd just turned onto the dirt road leading to Jesse's house. "I bet every camera crew in Los Angeles is here," Nancy said hopelessly.

It certainly looked that way. The little dirt road was crawling with people. Cars and camera trucks were parked all around the house. Reporters were thronging the front yard—and the hill in back was packed with spectators. The little house, all of its lights out, looked as though it was under siege.

"Oh, why can't they leave him alone!" Bess cried. "We don't have a chance of getting in to see him!"

"I'm afraid you're right, but we have to give it a try," Nancy said.

Just as the girls got out of the car, a roar went up from the crowd. Nancy turned quickly.

A light had just been turned on in Jesse's living room. Now the front door was opening a crack—and then all the way. And now Jesse was walking out onto the front step.

He stood there for a second, silent, making no attempt to shield his eyes from the glare of the flashes. "All right! All right! I'll tell you everything you want to know!" he shouted at the crowd.

At that exact moment a gunshot rang out—and Jesse Slade crumpled to the porch.

Chapter

Fourteen

ANOTHER SHOT ripped through the silence—
and then there was instant noise and pandemonium.

"We've got to help Jesse!" Nancy shouted to
Bess and George. But the screaming, panicky
mob that was now rushing away from the house
knocked her down before she could take a step.
Dizzily she struggled to her feet and forced
herself upright into the sea of elbows and knees.
At last she pushed her way to Jesse's front steps,
Bess and George right behind her.

Jesse was hunched over, covered with blood.
When he lifted his head, the skin on his face was
pulled tight with pain.

"Just—just my arm," he gasped. "Lucky. But get me inside."

Nancy was already moving. She, George, and Bess dragged him into the house and slammed the door. Just then a third shot rang out.

"Keep down, everybody!" Nancy ordered as she bolted the door. "Call the police, George—and tell them to bring an ambulance!"

She threw herself to the ground, slithered across the floor on her stomach, and lifted her head to peek cautiously out the window. On the road dozens of shrieking people were rushing to get into their cars. Nancy shuddered. Not all of them were driving away, but most of them were staying put, secure in their cars.

"Let's get you cleaned up, Jesse," she said briskly, turning away from the window. Quickly she tore his shirt open at the shoulder. Then she sighed with relief.

"You were right. It's only your arm," she said. "I can't get the bullet out, though—it's too deep. It must hurt incredibly."

"Burns," said Jesse through clenched teeth. "Who do you think is after me?"

"You'd know that better than I would," Nancy said as she hastily tied a strip of shirt around the wound. But Jesse just shook his head. She could tell that the effort of talking was too much for him.

"Nancy," said Bess in a trembling voice, "do

you realize we're trapped in here with a killer outside waiting for us?"

"Don't worry, Bess," said Nancy as calmly as she could. "The police should be here any minute."

"But what if he's right outside the door?"

"The door's locked. We've done everything we can. They'll be here before you know it," Nancy assured her friend. She only hoped it was true.

Jesse moaned. His lips were gray now, and his eyes kept rolling back in his head. Nancy checked his pulse. She could hardly feel it—and the bandage she'd put around his arm was already drenched in blood.

"They've got to get here soon," she repeated. "We've done everything we can."

But ten minutes crawled by before Nancy and her friends heard the welcome sound of the police siren.

"They're here!" Bess was almost sobbing with relief as she ran to the front door and yanked it open.

In just seconds the house was swarming with people. The reporters piled out of their cars and were furiously snapping pictures again. Two paramedics bundled Jesse onto a stretcher. They were pushing through the crowd to carry him out the door when Jesse whispered hoarsely, "Nancy," and stopped their progress.

"Here I am," she said, moving over to stand next to the stretcher.

"Where are you staying, in case I need to get in touch with you?" he asked, and Nancy told him the name of their hotel. "A friend of mine at TVR has a place where you can stay when you get out of the hospital," she added, "so you won't need to come back here if you don't want to."

He smiled. "I—don't," he whispered. His head was lolling sleepily to the side now.

"We'd better take him in, miss," said one of the paramedics. "You can call to see how he is later."

Jesse gripped Nancy's hand for a second, and then the paramedics carried him away.

Nancy felt tears stinging her eyes as she watched them load the stretcher onto the ambulance. What have I done to that poor guy? she thought. If I'd never come looking for him, this might never have happened! If only—

"Miss?" A police officer was standing at her elbow. "I'm Officer McIntyre. I wonder if I could get a statement from you."

When she'd told him everything, he shook his head. "Not much to go on in the way of suspects," he said.

"I do know of two possible suspects, though," Nancy said and told him about Renee and Vint.

"That's something, anyway," Officer McIntyre said. "I'll have someone track them down. But what about this Tommy Road? Do you really think he could still be alive?"

"I don't know. I just don't know," said Nancy.

Something flitted across her mind just then, but she didn't have time to identify it before it was gone. "That cliff was so steep I don't see how anyone could survive a fall from it. But I can't believe a body could disappear without a trace, either."

"Stranger things have happened," said the officer. He turned to a younger officer who'd just come in. "Yes, Rogers? What is it?"

"This, sir." The younger man held out his hand. "It's a spent rifle cartridge. We found it way up on the hill behind the house. No other signs of the gunman, though."

Or gunwoman, Nancy said to herself.

"Probably long gone," said Officer McIntyre. "But we'll post two guards here overnight, just to make sure." He turned to Nancy. "I'd like your number, in case I need to ask you anything more. Other than that, you and your friends are free to go."

In silence the three girls drove back through the dark to the hotel. Silent still, they parked the car in the garage, went into the bungalow, and sat down facing one another.

At last Nancy spoke. "We never got any supper," she said. "Anyone hungry?"

"I'm not, that's for sure," Bess said in a small voice. Then she burst into tears.

"I feel so terrible for Jesse!" she wept. "He's been through so much. And he's—he's not even like a real person any more. There's nobody inside. He's just a—a robot!"

"I feel bad, too," said George. "It was horrible to see someone who'd once been such a star living like *that*. I wish we'd never come here in the first place."

When Nancy spoke, it was as much to reassure herself as her friends. "Anybody would get a little strange living alone for so long—especially with that cliff scene in his past," she said. "He'll become himself again now that he's out in the real world again. He won't be able to help it. Someone that talented can't hide from things forever."

"As long as whoever's after him doesn't *get* him," George said darkly.

Nancy shivered. "That's the thing I do feel awful about," she said. "If we hadn't found him, the person with the rifle wouldn't have, either."

Then she squared her jaw and sat up straighter. "We'll have to catch that person, that's all," she said. "We started this, and we're going to finish it. But we need a good night's sleep first. I'd better call Ned. He'll be wondering what's happened to me."

"Hello?" came Ned's groggy voice after she'd dialed his number. She was using the phone next to her bed.

"Oh, Ned, I'm so sorry!" said Nancy, aghast. "I forgot about the time difference. I'll call you back tomorrow—"

"No, you won't. Talk to me now," said Ned. "I'm getting more awake every second. How's the case going?"

"Oh, Ned . . ." Nancy poured it all out to him, and when she was done she was almost in tears herself.

"This just isn't the way cases are supposed to go," she said in a wobbly voice. "I'm supposed to come in and solve them, and then everyone is happier and I can go home. But this time it seems as though I've only made things worse!"

"Not true," Ned said emphatically. "You've helped that guy, whether it seems like it now or not. And you'll catch whoever shot him—you always do, you know. I'm not even going to tell you to be careful this time. You just go out and *get* that gunman. But be careful," he added at the last minute.

Nancy giggled. "I love you, Ned. I feel a lot better now. I'm really glad I called—even if I did deprive you of your beauty sleep."

"Hey, I'm already gorgeous enough," Ned said lightly. "Now you go and get some beauty sleep yourself—not that you need it, either. And give me a call when you get a chance. I love you."

The phone woke her early the next morning.

"Nancy?" It was a man's voice, hoarse and hesitant, and for a second Nancy was too sleepy to recognize it.

"It's Jesse. I'm sorry to call you, but I didn't have anyone else to call."

"Hi, Jesse," Nancy said, struggling to sound alert. "How's your arm doing?"

His answer startled her. "The arm doesn't matter. Nancy, I'm in trouble. Really big trouble."

Nancy was wide-awake now. "What's the matter?" she asked.

"The matter is that there are two policemen standing at the foot of my bed right now. And they're here to arrest me!"

Chapter

Fifteen

Yes, I THINK we've finally got the proof we need," the police officer told Nancy. "It will be nice to see this case closed. I'm sorry for Slade, though. It doesn't look good for him."

Jesse had been so frightened by the sight of the police at the foot of his bed that he'd panicked. He hadn't been under arrest at all—the police had just wanted to ask him a few questions. But the direction the questions had led was all too clear to Nancy.

"Where's your evidence?" Nancy asked, controlling her anger.

When she'd finished talking to Jesse Nancy had woken George. Bess had been so sleepy that

Nancy had had to give up trying to rouse her. She'd left a note before she and George hurried into clothes and rushed off to the police station to see what was going on. Now they were talking to one of the men who'd questioned Jesse—Officer Squires, a tall, gangly man with an infuriatingly patronizing expression.

"We've got some very convincing evidence," he said. Nancy half expected him to add, "Young ladies." "Last night someone delivered us an anonymous package. I'm the one who opened it." For some reason he seemed quite proud of himself. "Inside there was a bloodstained T-shirt— and a note. Here's the note, if you'd like to see it. Careful not to touch it, though."

Nancy and George stared at the note. It had been scribbled in pencil on a torn sheet of notebook paper.

This shirt once belonged to Tommy Road, who was viciously murdered by Jesse Slade. I saw it happen and found the body. Slade's been hiding out all this time—but he can't get away from justice.

It was signed, "A Friend of the Law."

"But this is ridiculous!" Nancy protested. "There's no way to prove that the shirt is Tommy's—or that whoever wrote this note witnessed anything at all!"

"There's no way to prove it," agreed Officer

129

Squires. "But you may be interested in knowing that we did a lab check on the T-shirt. The blood type is the same as Tommy Road's. And the bloodstains are the right age."

He stared smugly at her, and for a second Nancy could think of nothing to say.

I know Tommy Road's not dead, she said to herself. I'm just sure of it. I've got to keep Jesse from going to trial for murder! But how do you explain a hunch to a police officer?

At last she found her voice. "As you say, that's interesting," she said. "But it can't be true—for a very simple reason. I know that Tommy Road is still alive." From the corner of her eye she could see George turning to stare at her, but she kept her gaze on Officer Squires.

"And just *how* do you know that?" he asked.

"I'm working on the evidence right now," Nancy replied. I'll find some, anyway, she thought. "And I'm sure that TV Rock will back me up. I'm heading right over to the station to bring one of their camera crews here."

To her secret satisfaction, Officer Squires was starting to look worried. "And now," Nancy asked, "where's Jesse? We'd like to talk to him."

"He's out of the hospital," the officer answered a little sullenly. "You can see him any time. He's waiting for you in there." He pointed to a door at the end of the room and turned his back on them. "I've got a lot of work to do," he muttered. "What a way to spend a Sunday morning."

Jesse was sitting on a bench, his head against the wall. He stood up when he saw them—and then winced. "I've got to remember to move more slowly," he said.

Under his shirt, his shoulder was bulging with bandages. "How's your arm?" George asked solicitously.

"Much better." He started to smile, but the smile faded instantly. "It'll have plenty of time to heal in jail, too."

"Don't talk that way!" Nancy said. "You're not under arrest. And we're going to beat this thing!"

"I'm glad to hear you say that, Nancy," George said, "and I can't wait to hear how. But let's talk about it outside. I don't want to turn around and find Officer Squires looming over me."

There was a little coffee shop next to the police station. Over coffee and doughnuts Nancy told George and Jesse about her hunch. Both of them looked at her doubtfully when she'd finished.

"It would be great if it were true," Jesse said, "but why are you so sure? Just because there's no body doesn't mean there wasn't a body once, if you know what I mean. Believe me, I'm not eager to face a murder rap, but I don't trust hunches."

"Nancy's hunches are *always* right," George said loyally. "And not because she's psychic or anything. She only gets hunches when she's noticed some little detail subconsciously. It's as if something trips her memory. That's why I'm sure she's right now. But how you're going to explain this to the police and Mr. Thomas, I just don't know."

"It's the shirt," Nancy said.

"Excuse me?" Jesse asked.

Nancy was frowning thoughtfully. "When you think about it, that bloody shirt doesn't make any sense," she said. "Let's just say it's true that there's a witness to the fight who doesn't want to get involved. Let's take it even further and say that the witness did hang onto the shirt all this time, hoping that when Jesse did turn up, he or she would be able to incriminate him. Okay, it's possible—barely.

"But it was a T-shirt! Can you imagine anyone who'd watch the fight, wade into the water to retrieve a body, take a bloody T-shirt off a *corpse,* and then decide just to leave the body in the water? It's not believable. It just doesn't make any sense! I don't think there was ever a dead body. I think Tommy Road survived the fall, kept his shirt, and only came forward now that Jesse's back."

"You know, you're right! That's just Tommy's style," said Jesse. He gave a giddy laugh. "I guess I'm not a murderer after all! Boy, I feel as though you've lifted a ten-ton weight off my head!"

"But we've still got to convince everyone else," Nancy said. She set her coffee cup down with a click. "Let's get over to TVR now. I'm going to call Mr. Thomas and ask him to meet us there."

"He's on his way," she said, returning from the pay phone. "He wasn't tremendously happy to be woken up this early on Sunday, but I told him it couldn't wait."

The TVR building was all but deserted. A sleepy-looking receptionist in the lobby winced when she saw them rushing in. "You look *much* too wide-awake," she said with a yawn. "Go on into Mr. Thomas's office. He's expecting you."

He was sitting behind his desk when they walked in, his fingers drumming the desktop impatiently. "This had better be good," he began —and then he saw Jesse.

His eyes widened. "Jesse Slade!" he exclaimed. "I thought you'd been arr—I mean, taken to hospital!"

Nancy was sure Mr. Thomas had been about to say "arrested." Now, how did he know that? she wondered. Did he find out about it on TV? But what news station could have gotten the story so quickly? Jesse had only been with the police for half an hour.

And why had he said "taken to hospital" instead of "taken to *the* hospital"?

The ghost of a suspicion was beginning to float around Nancy's brain. Could Winslow Thomas be British? Tommy Road had been British, too. . . .

Before she could think about it further, Mr.

Thomas jumped up with his hand extended. "I'm so pleased to make your acquaintance," he said rapidly. "On behalf of TVR, I'd like to welcome you back to the world."

"Nice to meet you," Jesse said. He was looking a little perplexed, Nancy thought. "We—we haven't met before, have we?"

"I wish we had," Winslow said regretfully. "But TVR hadn't really taken off when you—uh —vanished. I hope we'll have the pleasure of working together often from now on."

He turned to Nancy. "Was this why you had me come—to meet Jesse?"

"Not exactly," said Nancy. She took a deep breath. "Mr. Thomas, I've gone ahead and stuck my neck out on something. I hope you won't mind." And she described what had just taken place at the police station.

"You *what?*" Mr. Thomas asked, reddening angrily. "How could you involve this station in something so farfetched? That seems a little nervy to me, Nancy."

"I really had no choice." Nancy met his gaze steadily. "You see, I know I'm right."

Winslow Thomas's face was contorted with rage now. "I've never heard of such a thing! You wheedled your way in here, and now you're going to make a laughingstock of us! I should call the police and have you thrown out of here!"

What was happening to his accent? All of a

sudden it was British! Nancy looked at her friends and saw that they were as puzzled as she.

The hint that had been nagging her began to surface. Suddenly she realized it had to be true.

"Go on, get out!" he was shouting.

"You are Tommy Road!" Nancy whispered.

Mr. Thomas froze. "What—what are you saying?" he sputtered. *"You* really are crazy!"

"No, she's right!" Jesse gasped. "I *knew* I'd seen you before!"

"It's all starting to make sense now," Nancy said. "Your voice. The British phrases that kept popping out. Your weird-looking beard. And there was plenty of time for you to get over to Jesse's house last night, once I'd told you everything. You were the one who shot him. You must have been hanging around and watching to see what happened. You gave that shirt to the police. That's why you thought Jesse had been arrested!"

Mr. Thomas—Tommy Road—hesitated for a second. Then he gave her an ironic bow. "I must congratulate you," he said, his eyes full of hate. "I'm only surprised our friend Mr. Slade didn't recognize me sooner."

He wheeled around to turn his full fury on Jesse. "You tried to kill me," he spat out.

Jesse's face was white with shock. "I—I didn't! You know I didn't mean for you to fall off that cliff! It was an accident!"

"It may have been an accident," Tommy Road

said in a steely voice, "but you'll pay for it. When I'm done with you, you'll wish *you'd* been the one who'd slid off that cliff."

"You didn't even really manage to hurt me," he sneered. "I sprained my ankle, but that was about it. I watched you come down the cliff. I could tell it was too dark for you to see me. I swore I'd kill you when you reached the bottom. But when you took off down the beach, I thought —wait, this is my big chance!

"I assumed you'd report that I'd died. I hoped you'd be found guilty of my death. Whichever one happened, I knew no one would be trying to arrest Tommy Road for embezzlement. You can't arrest a dead man! It was my big chance to get away with the money and start a new life. I wouldn't even have to leave the country.

"Of course I saved my bloody shirt just in case it might come in handy someday," he continued. "And earlier that week—when I found out you'd been snooping around the accounts—I'd taken the precaution of switching the money in my account to a numbered Swiss account. No names necessary. All I had to do was grow a beard, wait until my hair grew in—and start life over. First I invested in record production. Then in music videos. And then I got my own music channel." He chuckled suddenly. "Of course I don't let any of the bands I used to handle perform on TVR."

Now he turned to Nancy. "You've obviously done a lot of thinking, Ms. Drew. It's a pity that you're so clever, because I'm not about to let *anyone* interfere with my plans. Not an amateur detective. Not a has-been rock star. Not *anyone!*"

And before anyone could stop him, he bolted from the room.

"We've got to catch him!" Nancy shouted.

The three of them dashed out of the office. Tommy Road was just disappearing into one of the preview rooms at the end of the hall. They pursued him to the door.

"It was this room," Nancy called, and they ran into it so fast that they piled up at the entrance.

The little room was pitch-dark. "Wait!" Nancy said. "He's not—"

There was a click—the sound of the door being locked.

Nancy whirled around to test the door they'd just come through. "He just locked it," she said.

Frantically Jesse rattled the knob of the door at the other end of the room. It was locked, too.

Then a light came on in the production booth on the other side of the glass wall. Tommy Road was sitting at the controls.

"Now that we're all gathered together, I've got a little number for your listening pleasure," he cooed into the microphone. "It's the first play of a song that I know will go gold. I know you're going to love it."

He smiled—and hit a switch in front of him.

A screeching blast filled the preview room. It was the same noise—the same unbearably loud noise—that Nancy had heard in her car. But now it was magnified a hundred times.

Nancy clapped her hands over her ears, but it was no use. Nothing could protect them against that deadly shriek.

Jesse collapsed to the floor, writhing. George looked as if she was screaming, but the evil blast was drowning out her voice.

So he's the one who rigged the car stereo, Nancy thought dazedly. It was all she could do to hold on to that thought. George had fallen to the floor, and Nancy knew she also was about to collapse.

The sound was killing them!

Chapter

Sixteen

AS SHE FELL to her knees, Nancy could see Tommy Road laughing maniacally. She reached her hand pleadingly out to him, but all he did was wag a teasing finger at her. He'd gone mad. He picked his suit jacket up off the chair next to him and strolled leisurely out of the control booth.

He's leaving us to die! Nancy thought desperately.

The preview room was soundproof. If there was anyone in the building, he or she couldn't hear the sound that was slowly draining the life out of Nancy and her friends. Nancy hurt so badly she couldn't move a muscle.

But she knew she had to try.

The electric guitar, Nancy ordered herself. Someone had left it there—she couldn't remember who. It was still leaning against the wall across the room.

With torturous slowness Nancy set out to crawl across the floor toward it. She felt like a diver whose last bit of air was gone, but she made herself move until she'd reached the wall.

Pick up the guitar, she ordered herself. She reached forward—but her hand wouldn't close.

Pick it up! she screamed at herself. And this time she did. Staggering, she dragged the guitar over to the sound booth and hoisted it into the air. With all the force she had, she hurled it at the glass separating them from the sound booth. Then she grabbed the window ledge and pulled herself up into the booth.

Her brain was screaming instructions at her. What switch? *What switch?* It had to be that one—the red one right in front of her. Feebly Nancy reached forward and flipped it.

The sound stopped, and a miraculous silence filled the room.

Nancy let out a long, shaky breath and collapsed into a chair. All she wanted to do was let the quiet soak into her.

On the floor in the preview room, George and Jesse were slowly uncurling and sitting up. To Nancy, both of them looked as though they were just coming out of a long, wrenching nightmare.

"Thanks, Nancy," Jesse said. He cleared his

throat. "Sorry I couldn't be more helpful. I really think that if that sound had gone on for one minute longer, I'd be dead now."

"I know I would have been," said George, and quickly shuddered. "I can't believe you've had to go through this twice, Nancy." She looked around. "I suppose it's no good hoping that Tommy Road is still around."

"No. He left a few minutes ago," Nancy said. "I'm sure he didn't hang around, either. He's probably off to plan some alibi."

"Do you mean he's going to get away with this?" George asked in horror.

"No, he's not," Nancy answered firmly. "What we need to do is think up a way to trap him. And I think I've got a perfect idea. Tommy Road has never seen Bess, has he? Well, then . . ."

Winslow Thomas's press conference at the Wilshire Hotel was attended by everyone who *was* anyone. The dozens of reporters packed into the room listened attentively as he described his feelings about Jesse Slade's return.

"To put it simply, I couldn't be more delighted," he said, "both for the music world and for TVR. This is a bloke with a tremendous talent who hasn't even begun to tap his potential in music videos. We're going to do great things together."

"Do you know Slade personally?" one reporter asked.

The flicker of a frown passed across Mr. Thomas's face and quickly vanished. "Of course I do," he said sincerely. "He's a fabulous, fabulous person. It wouldn't be putting it too strongly to say I love him."

"What about his legal problems, Mr. Thomas?" another reporter asked. "Will he be charged in Tommy Road's disappearance?"

"As far as I'm concerned, that problem doesn't exist," Mr. Thomas said graciously. "Of course we'll do all we can to help him if he *needs* help, but we're not interested in dragging up the past here. It's much more important to—"

"He's dead! Jesse's dead!" came a heartbroken wail from the doorway.

There was a gasp of shock. Everyone turned to see Bess standing by the door. Her face was contorted with grief and terror, and she was shaking from head to foot.

"They're all dead," she sobbed. "I—I went over to TVR, and they were all lying dead in one little room! Oh, Jesse!" And she burst into fresh tears.

It was Winslow Thomas's finest hour. As he listened to Bess, he actually grew white. Horror seemed to shrink him in his clothes. He groped blindly behind him for a chair and sank into it.

"What—what happened?" he asked hoarsely. "What do you mean, he's dead? How can that be?"

Bess wiped her eyes. All the cameras in the room were focused on her now.

"I—I went to TVR to pick up two friends," she choked out. "I couldn't find them anywhere, so I started looking up and down the hall. And in one of the rooms at the end, I—oh, it was too horrible!" She buried her face in her hands for a minute while the cameras clicked avidly. "I saw my friends and Jesse just lying there in a pool of broken glass!"

"Mr. Thomas" was clearly stricken. He rose tremblingly to his feet.

"Because of the tragic circumstances," he almost whispered, "I'd like to end this press conference immediately."

There was a murmur of sympathy through the room. Mr. Thomas tried to walk toward the door, but shock had made his legs too weak. Two men sprang to his aid, and—leaning heavily on their shoulders, the very image of a broken man—he staggered toward the door.

"Hi, Tommy," said Nancy breezily as she, George, and Jesse walked in right in front of him.

"Jesse!" It was a strangled scream—and Nancy knew that this time Tommy's horror was real.

"You're not here. You're not," he babbled. "None of you. No one could survive a noise like that—I made sure of it. You're dead. You've got to be dead."

"Why, Tommy," Jesse protested in a syrupy

143

voice, "don't you know that it would take more than a little rock 'n' roll to kill *me?* What do you take me for?"

Tommy Road just stared at him, transfixed. Then, for the first time, he realized that all the cameras in the room were still rolling. Screaming, he turned to run.

But he wasn't quick enough. Nancy tackled him like a ton of bricks—and the reporters were there to catch every detail.

Chapter

Seventeen

So Tommy Road has confessed to everything?"
Dan Kennedy asked.

It was the day after the press conference.
Nancy, Bess, and George were entertaining a few
visitors in their bungalow. Renee Stanley and
Vint Wylie were sitting next to each other on the
sofa. Dan Kennedy was lounging comfortably on
the floor. And Jesse Slade was sitting in an easy
chair that supported his bandaged arm.

Even with the bandages, Jesse already looked
like a different person. It wasn't only that he'd
shaved and bought himself some new clothes. "If
I'm going to pick up where I left off, I need to
dress the part," he'd told Nancy. And Bess had

145

had a wonderful time helping him shop. It was more a change in his expression. He no longer seemed beaten, lost, and withdrawn. Now he looked calm, relaxed, and confident. As George had teasingly told him, his star quality was back.

"Yes," Nancy told Dan. "He confessed to everything. Including spreading rumors at TVR that I was a spy from a rival video station."

"I sure fell for that one," said Renee, wincing. "He came in the night before I met you, Nancy, and told me that he'd hired you as a guest veejay because he thought that would be the best way to keep you from finding anything out. In fact, he *ordered* me to keep you from finding out anything. He told me it was fine to give you a hard time on the job—and he also told me to keep him posted on your schedule. It wasn't my fault that you're so quick on your feet." She smiled at Nancy, and Nancy smiled back.

"I'd kept wondering why Mr. Thomas insisted on making me go undercover and made me promise not to tell anyone," Nancy said. "Now I know that it was because he didn't want anyone to notice that his story and mine were so different. And now I know why everyone seemed so unfriendly that first day!"

"Did he plant that phony package for you, too?" asked Bess.

"Yes. Mr. Thomas—I mean Tommy—

managed to drop it off without the receptionist seeing, and then picked it up when she was off making the copies he'd asked her to do. While I was trying to track it down, he wired my car stereo."

Bess shivered. "I can't believe how lucky you were, Nan. What if you'd been driving on the freeway when that noise started up? You could have been killed!"

"Believe me, I thought of that," Nancy said dryly. "So could a lot of other people—but Tommy didn't care about that. He's *really* charming."

"What happens to him now?" George asked.

"Well, he'll be charged with embezzlement, of course," Nancy said, *"and* attempted murder. You know, he's claiming there's no evidence linking him to that little scene in the preview room. He's so convincing that I'd almost believe him myself. It's lucky he spilled the beans in front of a roomful of reporters."

"What about TVR?" Bess asked, and Dan smiled.

"I got the news about that this morning," he said. "Winslow's—I mean Tommy's—second-in-command will take over. She's really great. And I've been promoted, too—to head veejay."

"Congratulations!" Renee said, and she sounded as though she meant it. "That's great. It will be fun to work for you."

She cleared her throat nervously. "Nancy, you

know I owe you an apology—but at least I behaved badly to you because I thought you were out to sabotage the station. But there's another person here who deserves an apology, too. Jesse—I don't know what to say."

"I don't, either," said Vint. "We're just really sorry, Jesse. We didn't mean to hurt you."

"That's why I freaked out so much when I heard that you were still alive," Renee said. "I couldn't stand thinking that you'd find out I'd started seeing Vint. It seemed like one of those horribly sad movies where the hero goes to war or something, and when he gets back his girl-friend has married someone else . . ." She took out a tissue and blew her nose.

"Don't think about it," Jesse said. "It's all past tense now. You're two of my favorite people, and I'm glad you're together. Besides, my life-style for the past few years hasn't exactly been the kind of thing I'd want to make a girl share.

"Anyway, now that I'm going back into the rock-star biz I'll have lots of money again. And I'll be able to date all kinds of incredible girls," he added teasingly—then dodged as Renee hurled a throw pillow at his head.

"What are you planning to do, Nancy?" Renee asked.

"Oh, we're heading home," Nancy told her.

"You know, you don't *have* to leave right away," said Dan. "I found out something inter-esting just before I came over here. It seems that guest-veejay interview you did was a big hit. We've been getting a lot of calls about it— everyone wants to see you on TVR again. Any chance you'd consider taking a job with us?"

"You're kidding!" Nancy gasped. "Me, a veejay? That's great! I mean, it's a great compliment. But, Dan, I'm a detective. I *like* being a detective. I like my life in River Heights. Thanks, though."

"Well, couldn't the three of you stay a little longer just for a vacation?" Dan asked. "As head veejay, I have an even bigger expense account now. I'd be more than happy to put you up at the hotel a little longer. And I could make some time to show you the sights, too."

Nancy looked at Bess and George. They all shook their heads.

"It's a tempting offer. Maybe we could take you up on it in a couple of months. But I want to go home for now," George said. "All I seem to do is sit in cars here."

"I'd love to come back here someday, but I want to go home, too," said Bess. "But I'll watch you every day, Dan. And Jesse, I expect you to write at *least* one song about all this."

He smiled at her. "It'll be dedicated to you, Bess," he said, and Bess giggled happily.

"I have to go home, too," said Nancy. "I miss Ned too much—and besides, there are sure to be other cases waiting for me back in River Heights."

"But they won't be as *glamorous* as this one was, will they?" Renee teased her.

"I hope not!" Nancy said fervently. "I've had enough of the glamorous music world to last me a lifetime. From now on, I'm sticking to plain, ordinary, uncomplicated everyday life."

But no one in the room believed her for a second.

Nancy's next case:

As a favor to Ned, Nancy goes undercover at a River Heights hospital. Trevor Callahan, a young doctor, is being blamed for his future father-in-law's sudden death after heart surgery. But before Nancy can investigate, the body is stolen!

When the teen detective starts work in the emergency room, she soon finds every moment is vital. A mysterious killer is stalking the wards, and Nancy is high on the critical list. If she fails to diagnose the clues, her own life will need intensive care. And chances are the young sleuth won't survive the treatment . . . in *BAD MEDICINE*, Case #35 in the Nancy Drew Files™.

Forthcoming Titles in the
Nancy Drew Files™ Series

Gung-ho missions and tense, rollicking investigations – **The Hardy Boys** ™ are unstoppable! And now Simon & Schuster Ltd. are publishing two thrilling titles every month.

The Hardy Boys ™ are back! Frank and Joe don't court danger, it just happens along. As private investigators they ricochet from case to case, investigating, troubleshooting and putting gross wrongs to right. These two young detectives dance with death and untangle dangerous schemes in a series of hard-paced, fast-moving, action-packed adventures.

Books in The Hardy Boys™ Casefiles Series

Simon & Schuster publish a wide range of titles from pre-school books to books for adults.

For up-to-date catalogues, please contact:

International Book Distributors
Campus 400
Maylands Avenue
Hemel Hempstead
Herts
HP2 7EZ

Tel. 0442 882255